Maple turned her arm into tentacles,
ripping chunks off the squid and
swallowing them. Mai and Yui each
slammed eight hammers home.

"You wanna c— Uh, would you like to join me?"

Velvet suggested, brushing off her slip with a smile. Mii shot her a look of envy.

"I had no other plans. I shall accompany you."

On a quiet seventh-stratum hill

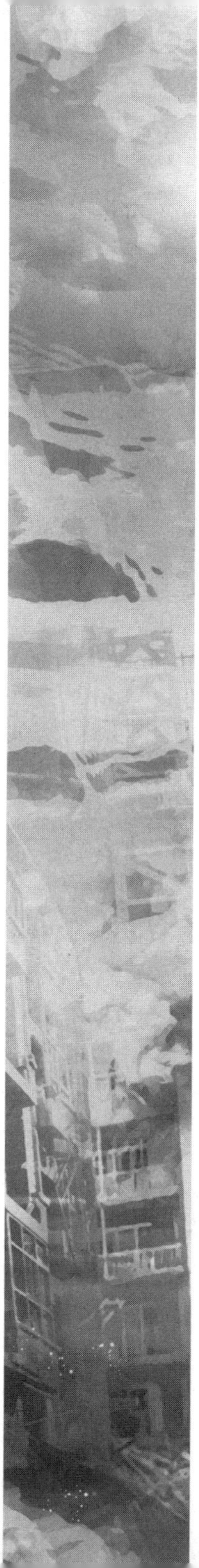

Skills

Magic Mastery X / Magic Secrets VIII / Fast Chant
Multi-Cast / Mana Fountain / MP Ocean / Fire Magic VIII
Water Magic VIII / Wind Magic VIII / Earth Magic VIII
Dark Magic VI / Light Magic X / MP Boost (L) / MP Cost Down (L)
MP Recovery Speed Boost (L) / Magic Boost (L)
Power Boost / Spell Boost / Mana Amp / Reinforced Magic
Poison Nullification / Paralyze Nullification / Stun Resist (L)
Sleep Resist (L) / Freeze Resist (M) / Burn Resist (L)
Fight Song / Incite

Bofuri
I Don't Want to Get Hurt, so I'll Max Out My Defense.

11

YUUMIKAN

Illustration by KOIN

FREDERICA'S STATS

Frederica

Lv80	HP ???/???	MP ??/??
[STR ??]	[VIT ??]	[AGI ??]
[DEX ??]	[INT ??]	⚠SECRET⚠

Welcome to
NewWorld Online.

YEN ON
NEW YORK

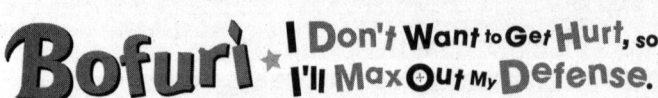

YUUMIKAN

Translation by Andrew Cunningham • Cover art by Koin

ITAINO WA IYA NANODE BOGYORYOKU NI KYOKUFURI SHITAITO OMOIMASU. Vol. 11
©Yuumikan, Koin 2021
First published in Japan in 2021 by KADOKAWA CORPORATION, Tokyo.
English translation rights arranged with KADOKAWA CORPORATION, Tokyo, through TUTTLE-MORI AGENCY, INC., Tokyo.

Yen On
150 West 30th Street, 19th Floor
New York, NY 10001

Visit us at yenpress.com • facebook.com/yenpress • twitter.com/yenpress
yenpress.tumblr.com • instagram.com/yenpress

First Yen On Edition: December 2023
Edited by Yen On Editorial: Leilah Labossiere, Ivan Liang
Designed by Yen Press Design: Liz Parlett

Yen On is an imprint of Yen Press, LLC.
The Yen On name and logo are trademarks of Yen Press, LLC.

Library of Congress Cataloging-in-Publication Data
Names: Yuumikan, author. I Koin, illustrator. I Cunningham, Andrew, 1979– translator.
Title: Bofuri, I don't want to get hurt, so I'll max out my defense / Yuumikan ; illustration by Koin ; translated by Andrew Cunningham.
Other titles: Itai no wa iya nano de bōgyoryoku ni kyokufuri shitai to omoimasu. English
Description: First Yen On edition. I New York : Yen On, 2021–
Identifiers: LCCN 2020055872 I ISBN 9781975322731 (v. 1 ; trade paperback) I
    ISBN 9781975323547 (v. 2 ; trade paperback) I ISBN 9781975323561 (v. 3 ; trade paperback) I
    ISBN 9781975323585 (v. 4 ; trade paperback) I ISBN 9781975323608 (v. 5 ; trade paperback) I
    ISBN 9781975323622 (v. 6 ; trade paperback) I ISBN 9781975323646 (v. 7 ; trade paperback) I
    ISBN 9781975323660 (v. 8 ; trade paperback) I ISBN 9781975323684 (v. 9 ; trade paperback) I
    ISBN 9781975367688 (v. 10 ; trade paperback) I ISBN 9781975367701 (v. 11 ; trade paperback)
Subjects: LCSH: Video gamers—Fiction. I Virtual reality—Fiction. I GSAFD: Science fiction.
Classification: LCC PL874.I46 I8313 2021 I DDC 895.63/6—dc23
LC record available at https://lccn.loc.gov/2020055872

ISBNs: 978-1-9753-6770-1 (paperback)
       978-1-9753-6771-8 (ebook)

10 9 8 7 6 5 4 3 2 1

LSC-C

Printed in the United States of America

CONTENTS

I Don't Want to Get Hurt,
so I'll Max Out My Defense.

NewWorld Online Status ‖ GUILD **Maple Tree**

‖ NAME **Maple** LV **64**

HP 200/200   MP 22/22

PROFILE
The Tankiest Great Shielder

She was a gaming noob, but by putting all her points in defense, she grew so tanky that all attacks just bounce right off. The kind of girl who finds fun in everything, her imaginative leaps astound those around her. When she fights, she negates all incoming attacks while unleashing a barrage of counter-skills.

STATUS
【STR】 000 【VIT】 17550 【AGI】 000
【DEX】 000 【INT】 000

EQUIPMENT
‖ New Moon: Hydra   ‖ Bonding Bridge

‖ Night's Facsimile: Devour/Lure of the Deep

‖ Black Rose Armor: Saturating Chaos

‖ Toughness Ring   ‖ Life Ring

SKILLS
Shield Attack   Sidestep   Deflect   Meditation   Taunt   Inspire   HP Boost (S)   MP Boost (S)   Heavy Body

Green's Grace   Great Shield Mastery VIII   Cover Move IV   Cover   Pierce Guard   Counter   Quick Change

Absolute Defense   Moral Turpitude   Sheep Eater   Hydra Eater   Bomb Eater   Indomitable Guardian

Giant Killing   Psychokinesis   Fortress   Martyr's Devotion   Machine God   Bug Urn Curse   Zone Freeze

Pandemonium I   Heaven's Throne   Nether Nexus   Crystallization   Cataclysmic Eruption   Unbreakable Shield

Twisted Resurrection   Earth Wielding II

TAMED MONSTER
‖ Name **Syrup**   A turtle with high defense

Giganticize   Spirit Cannon   Mother Nature   etc.

Don't Want to Get Hurt, so I'll Max Out My Defense

Welcome to *NewWorld Online*

NewWorld Online Status ║ GUILD **Maple Tree**

║ NAME **Sally**   LV **66**

HP 32/32   MP 130/130

PROFILE
The Unhittable Assassin

Maple's friend and partner, she's got a good head on her shoulders. Her top priority is to ensure she and Maple enjoy the game together. Light armor and twin daggers are the core of her combat style; her raw gaming talent and astonishing focus allow her to evade all attacks.

STATUS

STR 130 VIT 000 AGI 180
DEX 045 INT 060

EQUIPMENT

║ Deep Sea Dagger   ║ Seabed Dagger
║ Surface Scarf: Mirage   ║ Oceanic Coat: Oceanic
║ Oceanic Clothes   ║ Bonding Bridge
║ Charnel Boots: One Step in the Grave

SKILLS

Gale Slash   Defense Break   Inspire   Down Attack   Power Attack   Switch Attack   Pinpoint Attack
Combo Blade V   Martial Arts VIII   Fire Magic III   Water Magic III   Wind Magic III   Earth Magic III
Dark Magic III   Light Magic III   Strength Boost (L)   Combo Boost (L)   MP Boost (M)   MP Cost Down (M)
MP Recovery Speed Boost (M)   Poison Resist (S)   Gathering Speed Boost (S)   Dagger Mastery X
Magic Mastery III   Dagger Secrets I   Affliction VIII   Presence Block III   Presence Detect II
Sneaky Steps I   Leap V   Quick Change   Cooking I   Fishing   Swimming X   Diving X   Shearing
Superspeed   Ancient Ocean   Chaser Blade   Jack of All Trades   Sword Dance   Shed Skin
Web Spinner VII   Ice Pillar   Subzero Domain   Nether Nexus   Cataclysmic Eruption   Water Wielding V
Substitute

TAMED MONSTER

║ Name **Oboro**   A fox with skills that bewilder foes

Fleeting Shadow   Shadow Clone   Binding Barrier   etc.

Don't Want to Get Hurt, so I'll Max Out My Defense

Welcome to NewWorld Online

NewWorld Online Status

▍GUILD **Maple Tree**

▍NAME Chrome   ▍LV **84**

HP 940/940   **MP** 52/52

PROFILE
The Unstoppable, Unyielding Zombie Tank

Known as a top player since the early days of *NewWorld Online*. Reliable, looks after people, everyone's big brother. Like Maple, he's a Great Shielder. His unique gear gives him a 50 percent chance of surviving any hit with 1 HP, and he has a ton of healing skills that make him extremely tenacious.

STATUS
STR 140 **VIT** 180 **AGI** 040
DEX 030 **INT** 020

EQUIPMENT
▍Headhunter: Life Eater

▍Wrath Wraith Wall: Soul Syphon

▍Bloodstained Skull: Soul Eater

▍Bloodstained Bone Armor: Dead or Alive

▍Robust Ring   ▍Impregnable Ring

▍Bonding Bridge

SKILLS
Thrust   Elemental Blade   Shield Attack   Sidestep   Deflect   Great Defense   Taunt   Bulwark
Impregnable Stance   Iron Body   Guardian   Heavy Body   HP Boost (L)   HP Recovery Speed Boost (L)   Cover
MP Boost (L)   Green's Grace   Great Shield Mastery X   Defense Mastery X   Cover Move X   Pierce Guard
Counter   Guard Aura   Defensive Formation   Guardian Power   Great Shield Secrets IX   Defense Secrets VII
Burn Resist (L)   Stun Nullification   Paralyze Nullification   Poison Nullification   Sleep Nullification
Freeze Nullification   Mining IV   Gathering VII   Shearing   Spirit Light   Indomitable Guardian
Battle Healing   Reaper's Mire   Crystallization   Stimulation

TAMED MONSTER
▍Name **Necro**   An armor monster that really shines when worn

Polterguard   Impact Reflection   etc.

Don't Want to Get Hurt, so I'll Max Out My Defense
Welcome to *NewWorld Online*

NewWorld Online Status ‖ GUILD **Maple Tree**

‖ NAME **Iz** LV **69**

HP 100/100 MP 100/100

PROFILE
The Ultimate Crafter

A specialized crafter, she's proud of her work and particular about the results. Her gaming style is all about making clothes, weapons, armor, and items. Originally, she wasn't that active in combat, but her stock of attack and support items now makes a huge difference.

STATUS

STR 045 VIT 020 AGI 080

DEX 210 INT 085

EQUIPMENT

‖ Blacksmith Hammer X

‖ Alchemist Goggles: Faustian Alchemy

‖ Alchemist Long Coat: Magic Workshop

‖ Blacksmith Leggings X

‖ Alchemist Boots: New Frontier ‖ Potion Pouch

‖ Item Pouch ‖ Bonding Bridge

SKILLS

Strike Crafting Mastery X Crafting Secrets X Enhance Success Rate Boost (L) Gathering Speed Boost (L)

Mining Speed Boost (L) Crafting Quantity Boost (L) Crafting Speed Boost (L) Affliction III Sneaky Steps V

Keen Sight Smithing X Sewing X Horticulture X Synthesizing X Augmentation X Cooking X Mining X

Gathering X Swimming VII Diving VIII Shearing Godsmith's Grace X Observer's Eye Attribute Endowment VI

Botany Mineralogy

TAMED MONSTER

‖ Name **Fey** A spirit that helps with item creation

Item Boost Recycle etc.

Don't Want to Get Hurt, so I'll Max Out My Defense

Welcome to *NewWorld Online*

NewWorld Online Status ‖ GUILD **Maple Tree**

‖ NAME **Kasumi**　 LV **81**

HP 435/435　MP 70/70

PROFILE
The Solitary Sword Dancer

A katana-wielding female player with a strong knack for solo play. Always calm, she's good at assessing the big picture. Yet she's frequently left reeling by Maple's and Sally's outlandish antics. Has a range of katana skills that let her contribute to almost any combat situation.

STATUS
[STR] 205　[VIT] 080　[AGI] 105
[DEX] 030　[INT] 030

EQUIPMENT
‖ Yukari, the All-Consuming Blight

‖ Cherry Blossom Barrette

‖ Cherry Blossom Vestments

‖ Edo Purple Hakama　　‖ Samurai Greaves

‖ Samurai Gauntlets　　‖ Gold Obi Fastener

‖ Cherry Blossom Crest　‖ Bonding Bridge

SKILLS

Gleam　Helmsplitter　Guard Break　Sweep Slice　Eye for Attack　Inspire　Attack Stance　Katana Arts X　Cleave　Throw　Power Aura　Armor Slicer　HP Boost (L)　MP Boost (M)　Attack Boost (L)　Poison Nullification　Paralyze Nullification　Stun Resist (L)　Sleep Resist (L)　Freeze Resist (M)　Burn Resist (L)　Longsword Mastery X　Katana Mastery X　Longsword Secrets VI　Katana Secrets VII　Mining IV　Gathering VI　Diving V　Swimming VI　Leap VII　Shearing　Keen Sight　Indomitable　Sword Spirit　Dauntless　Sinew　Superspeed　Ever Vigilant　Mind's Eye　Specter of Carnage

TAMED MONSTER

‖ Name **Haku**　　A white snake that ambushes foes from the mist

Supergiant　Paralytoxin　etc.

Don't Want to Get Hurt, so I'll Max Out My Defense
Welcome to NewWorld Online

NewWorld Online Status

GUILD **Maple Tree**

NAME **Kanade** LV **57**

HP 335/335 MP 250/250

PROFILE
The Whimsical Genius Mage

A certifiable genius with an androgynous look and a memory beyond compare. His mind once left him avoiding human contact, but Maple's innocent cheer broke through that shell. He can store all manner of spells in the grimoires on his book stacks, ready for use in combat.

STATUS
STR **015** VIT **010** AGI **090**
DEX **050** INT **120**

EQUIPMENT
Divine Wisdom: Akashic Records
Diamond Newsboy Cap VIII
Smart Coat VI | Smart Leggings VIII
Smart Boots VI | Spade Earrings
Mage Gloves | Bonding Bridge

SKILLS
Magic Mastery VIII | Fast Chant | MP Boost (L) | MP Cost Down (L) | MP Recovery Speed Boost (L)
Magic Boost (M) | Green's Grace | Fire Magic VII | Water Magic V | Wind Magic VII | Earth Magic V
Dark Magic III | Light Magic VII | Sorcerer's Stacks | Reaper's Mire | Magic Meld

TAMED MONSTER
Name **Sou**   A slime that can copy a player's abilities
Mimic | Divide | etc.

Don't Want to Get Hurt, so I'll Max Out My Defense
Welcome to NewWorld Online

NewWorld Online Status ‖ GUILD **Maple Tree**

‖ NAME **Mai** LV **52**

HP 35/35 MP 20/20

PROFILE
Conquerer Twin

A beginner player with an extreme attack build, she and her younger twin sister, Yui, were scouted by Maple. She does her best to help everyone out. The twins have the highest DPS in the game, and their dual-wielding hammers vaporize anything that gets close.

STATUS

[STR] 505 [VIT] 000 [AGI] 000
[DEX] 000 [INT] 000

EQUIPMENT

‖ Black Annihilammer X ‖ Black Doll Dress X
‖ Black Doll Tights X ‖ Black Doll Shoes X
‖ Little Ribbon ‖ Silk Gloves
‖ Bonding Bridge

SKILLS

Double Stamp ・ Double Impact ・ Double Strike ・ Attack Boost (L) ・ Hammer Mastery X
Throw ・ Farshot ・ Conqueror ・ Annihilator ・ Giant Killing ・ Destroy Mode ・ Titan's Lot

TAMED MONSTER

‖ Name **Tsukimi** A bear monster with distinctive black fur

Power Share ・ Bright Star ・ etc.

Don't Want to Get Hurt, so I'll Max Out My Defense
Welcome to *NewWorld Online*

NewWorld Online Status ‖ GUILD **Maple Tree**

‖ NAME **Yui** LV **52**

HP 35/35   MP 20/20

PROFILE
Annihilator Twin

A beginner player with an extreme attack build, she and her older twin sister, Mai, were scouted by Maple. She's more positive than Mai and quicker to recover. The twins have the highest DPS in the game. Throwing Iz's custom-made iron balls lets them take out enemies at range.

STATUS

[STR] 505 [VIT] 000 [AGI] 000
[DEX] 000 [INT] 000

EQUIPMENT

‖ White Annihilammer X   ‖ White Doll Dress X
‖ White Doll Tights X   ‖ White Doll Shoes X
‖ Little Ribbon   ‖ Silk Gloves
‖ Bonding Bridge

SKILLS

Double Stamp   Double Impact   Double Strike   Attack Boost (L)   Hammer Mastery X
Throw   Farshot   Conqueror   Annihilator   Giant Killing   Destroy Mode   Titan's Lot

TAMED MONSTER

‖ Name **Yukimi**   A bear monster with distinctive white fur

Power Share   Bright Star   etc.

Don't Want to Get Hurt, so I'll Max Out My Defense
Welcome to NewWorld Online

Prologue

All the guilds flexed their might in the epic eighth event—but this was followed by a lull. As all *NewWorld Online* players waited for the eighth stratum to arrive, they found ways to enjoy the downtime. Boosting their levels or exploring new dungeons—everyone just did whatever they felt like doing.

Maple and Sally spent some time sightseeing on older floors. They observed what had changed in their old haunts on the first and second stratums and discovered new places they'd never been before. Every map in the game was vast, and they'd often rushed through the content. That left plenty of areas completely unexplored.

They checked out a flying castle, delved into a cavern, climbed a snow-capped peak, and admired the scenic views. And along the way, they teamed up with the masters of two other guilds.

The first guild master they met was Velvet, a specialist in powerful lightning attacks who leads Thunder Storm. Her partner was Hinata, an expert in debuffs utilizing an impressive array of ice and gravity spells. Maple and Sally cleared a dungeon with them, becoming friends—and rivals.

The second guild was Rapid Fire, led by Lily and Wilbert. By swapping their gear, these two could trade offensive and supporting roles. Both excelled at ranged attacks—Lily's summons could put up massive barrages, and Wilbert's bow could land high-powered attacks on individual targets with uncanny accuracy. Their strategies took full advantage of both skill sets.

Maple and Sally had made quite a name for themselves in previous events, so these emerging guilds clearly saw them as competition.

Since Maple had gone buck wild and hogged the limelight, quite a few of her abilities were public knowledge. Everyone assumed rivals would strategize against them, and she'd be at a disadvantage in PvP.

The two new rival guilds had skills that targeted not only Maple's weaknesses, but Sally's, too. They were legitimate threats.

Yet none of that really bothered Maple. She was just out doing her thing, picking up new skills, and getting stronger in ways no one could predict. As the game changed around our dynamic duo, the ninth event arrived.

CHAPTER 1

Defense Build and the Ninth Event

On the first day of the ninth event, Maple, Sally, and the rest of Maple Tree met in their guild home to discuss the event's format.

"No PvP elements. The whole player base will cooperate to see how many of the event-limited monsters they can kill."

"Oh, one of *those*. Well, if we're all in it together, we've gotta do our part!"

"Ha-ha-ha, just take it at your own pace. Plenty of people get way too into this sort of thing."

The third event had been a while back but had followed the same format. Several guilds had racked up kill counts far above the norm. They'd likely step up again.

"That being said, there are rewards for hitting specific kill counts, and if we make it all the way through, we'll get items that'll be useful on the eighth stratum. And the typical medals and money…"

"Oh! Then we're definitely gonna go all out."

"Yup. This event lasts awhile, and the event monsters will show up on any floor, so you can hunt them wherever you want."

"Then we've got a clear goal in mind. I guess I'll start by figuring out how many I can manage in a day."

"Yep, maybe it'll turn out to be pretty easy."

"I doubt the goals are all that steep. I'm mostly after the materials these things drop."

Chrome, Iz, and Kasumi agreed to keep an eye on what other players were doing, kill what they found, and focus on the monster drops.

"Yui, what should we do?"

"Um…if it's the same no matter where we are, let's go somewhere easy."

"Yeah, we don't really need levels right now."

The twins' HP was so low, they'd die if they took a hit no matter where they were. With no real reason to be competitive, they decided to play it safe and enjoy the event on their own terms.

"I think I'll take it slow, too," Kanade said. "If I get a chance, I'll scope out the rest of the player base. Maple and Sally were worried about future PvP."

"……! Yeah, that'll help a lot."

"Just don't get your hopes up," he said, grinning.

Since there was no competitive aspect to it, no one seemed inclined to get serious about the ninth event. Each set their own goals, determined to play their own way.

"Report in if you discover anything cool. All stratums are in play, and there's several types of monsters to hunt."

"Yeah, if one type turns out to drop good materials, I'd appreciate you prioritizing those."

Once an event like this ended, there was no telling if they'd ever see those monsters again. Iz wanted to stockpile as many drops as she could.

"Okay, let's just keep in touch!" Maple said.

Everyone agreed to share what they learned, then went out to confirm what stratums had which monsters.

Since the event itself was simple, Maple and Sally headed straight from the meeting to the field. They were both more than capable of soloing anything on the seventh stratum—the highest-level monsters currently implemented—so they focused their attention there, letting other guild members check out the lower floors.

Like always, Sally readied her horse, and then Maple clambered on behind her. They galloped across the fields and soon spotted some monsters they'd never encountered before.

"Those look like the fish I summon."

"That's them, right?"

"Yep, those are definitely the event monsters."

A school of fish was swimming through the air above the regular map. No such monsters were ordinarily found on dry land, so it was immediately obvious they were event-limited. On the seventh stratum, they'd hunt these to rack up their kill count.

"These aren't the only type out there; stronger ones might drop rare materials."

"Then we'll beat them all!"

"But since the goal is for total kills, let's go somewhere without other players."

"That does sound more efficient!"

"Yep. Supposedly these monsters show up *everywhere*."

Since this event was for the entire player base, the required kill tallies were quite high. The event lasted awhile, but people with limited play time—like Maple and Sally—would just have to pick away at that count when they could. So close to town, the unusually large crowds would just end up stealing one another's kills. It would be better if they moved toward the edge of the map.

After a long ride, they found themselves in a wasteland strewn with boulders. The location had an open line of sight but no particularly weird enemies or traps. It was a solid grinding spot. Sally hopped off her horse, helped Maple down, and had the horse wait nearby.

"Okay! Let's go find some."

"If we search a bit and aren't finding many, we can always move."

"True!"

But they didn't have to search long before they stumbled across the event monsters. A school of tropical fish swam across the sky, wreathed in blue light, very much like the fish summoned by Sally's Ancient Ocean skill.

"Let's see what they're made of!"

"Yep! Go for broke!"

Sally cloned herself and darted forward, while Maple deployed her artillery. They weren't holding back—going all out like this made it seem like they were up against a boss. These monsters might be event-limited, but they were no bigger than your standard tropical fish, and their only attacks seemed to be some mild sprays of water.

Against the two girls, their lives were but candles in the wind.

Sally easily dodged the water projectiles, and Maple's lasers just vaporized them. In the blink of an eye, the school of fish was reduced to dust.

"…Weaker than I expected. Given how high the target number is, I guess that makes sense."

"Yeah. That was a cakewalk!"

These two were among the strongest of the game's front-runners, and monsters designed for the game's typical player simply didn't pose a threat.

"I guess we just keep taking them out!"

"Sure, why not? But if we keep killing them this fast, the spawn rates may not keep up with us. The rest of the guild are hunting elsewhere, so once we've had our fill here, we could go see how they're doing."

"Okay! But first, let's make sure to hunt our fair share!"

They'd made short work of their first encounter, so they kept right on killing. The monsters knew Maple's guns and Sally's slashes could chew right through them, so they attacked on sight. As their kill count rose, something new appeared before them.

"Sally, is that a special monster, too?"

"Looks like. They did say there were several types."

Peering around the rocks, they could see another flying aquatic creature—a shark that was bigger than both girls combined.

They'd taken out several schools of fish, but this was their first shark.

"Are all the event monsters fishy?"

"Could be. It might drop something good, so no reason not to take a run at it."

"Okay! First shot's mine!"

Maple aimed a cannon around the rock, firing a beam at the shark.

Her aim proved true, and she scored a clean hit on the shark's torso, but it proved tougher than the tropical fish—its HP went down, but not fatally. Instead, its jaws opened wide, and it charged at them.

"One more! Whoaaaaa?!"

As Maple tried to fire again, a jet of water shot out of the ground, knocking her over. Realizing the shark was not the only threat, Sally tried to back off—and without getting up, Maple moved to defend her.

"Cover!"

She'd used this skill so often, the timing was instinctual by now.

7

Her quick thinking ensured Sally's safety, and an instant later, a geyser shot Maple skyward. Keeping an eye on Maple's trajectory, Sally dashed toward the shark.

"My turn!"

As she closed in, the shark tried to catch her in its jaws, but she slipped right past, slashing its sides and moving safely away. As she turned to make her next run, a voice called down from above.

"Sally! Keep it still!"

"Oboro, Binding Barrier!"

Sally wasted no time locking down the shark. Maple wouldn't call out like that without a good reason.

A moment later, there was a boom up above, and a black mass dropped onto the shark's head.

It was Maple, using Machine God to turn one arm into a giant sword.

With the shark immobilized, Maple had little trouble lopping off the shark's head. It rolled away from the body, leaving Maple with her sword jammed in the ground. She lost her balance, the blade snapped, and she went tumbling.

"Y-you okay…? Of course you are."

Sally hadn't seen that attack coming and was a little rattled, but she'd seen Maple fight often enough to know mere gravity wouldn't hurt her.

"I was just gonna fall like usual, but I figured I should put it to good use! Glad it worked out!"

"Most people don't fall as often as you do."

It was an idea Maple had dreamed up only because she spent so much time blowing herself sky-high. This game had fall damage, so ordinarily drops like that were too risky. Any other player's top priority would be finding a way to avoid hurting themselves.

"Oh, did it drop anything?"

Maple scrambled up and looked around. There was a lump of water on the ground—like some sort of slime.

"Is that it?"

"Wow! What's it for?"

Maple scooped it up and checked it out. The item details only described it as water imbued with mana. Crafting was hardly their territory, so they had no clue what it was or how it could be used.

"Uh…guess we pass this on to Iz. If it's worth her while, we'll want to find more, so the sooner the better."

The shark was likely rare, and they wouldn't stumble across them as often as the tropical fish. If this drop was valuable, they'd need to switch up their approach to find as many sharks as possible.

"Then let's go ask! No time like the present!"

"Aye-aye. We've mostly swept this area free of event monsters anyway. Chrome's crew is out exploring, but Iz has that skill that lets her use her workshop anywhere."

Sally sent Iz a message and then put Maple on her horse.

"We know the fish are small fry, so let's just hit them in passing as we go. I'll watch to see if they drop anything."

"Gotcha! I'll just blast away!"

They headed off to Iz, racking up more kills on the way.

Meanwhile, Chrome, Kasumi, and Iz were elsewhere on the seventh stratum. They had Haku Giganticized and were riding around on its head, killing event monsters as they went.

"Oh, Maple and Sally are headed our way. Seems they got a mystery drop from a rare monster."

"Nice. All we're seeing are these tropical fish."

They were using Haku's bulk to their advantage, doing circuits of the area and cleaning up the schools of fish. But those had yet to drop anything of note, and they'd yet to encounter any other monster types. Since they'd found only tropical fish and had no clue what else was out there, they were playing it safe. Iz might have skills that let her fight on the front lines now, but she needed a lot of setup to take advantage of them.

"The event monsters may be weak, but they're not exactly replacing the regular monsters. It's still risky for me to go it alone."

"I think you'd probably do just fine. You can make those cannons and all. As long as you get them out in time, you can solo most things."

"But items aren't *free*. They're not like skills where all you need to worry about is cooldown time."

Iz had a point, but it was also true that she could now fend for herself. She'd proved that by qualifying for the highest difficulty on the last event.

"This is all adding to our kill count, but what we're seeing seems trivial."

"Yeah, we're just mowing through them. But if we're after materials, easy is good. If we want a challenge, we can always find a stronger enemy or player instead."

"Hmm…I guess."

Best to take it easy when they could. Kasumi sent Haku through the next school, running them over, biting them out of the air, and steadily adding to their score.

And as Haku slithered its way to dominance, Maple and Sally caught up.

"Yo!"

"Ah, you're here? Haku, stop."

Kasumi had Haku lower its head to ground level.

"No problems, I trust?"

"Nope! We killed a bunch more from horseback on the way."

"You're doing just fine, then?"

"Yeah, with enemies this fragile, we don't have to worry."

"So…what's up, Maple?"

"Lookee here! Iz, for you!"

Maple passed over the lump of water. The moment Iz had her hands on the new material, she checked to see what new crafts became available.

"Um…looks like I can make items that extend your time underwater. Much more powerful than what I've been making, so that should help a lot with underwater exploration."

"Interesting… There are lots of lakes and oceans in this game. Could be handy!"

Maple was nodding. Sally had guessed it would make water-related items, and based on what Iz said, that was pretty much right on the money.

"Like I said, no telling when we can get more of these. Might be best if we focus on monsters other than the tropical fish."

"Yeah, that's probably a good idea. The total kill count's doing just fine."

As predicted, there were plenty of players racking up kills even faster than Kasumi's group. The total was well on its way toward the ultimate goal. It wouldn't hurt if Maple Tree prioritized the search for rare materials.

"Understood. With Haku, we don't even have to try. The small fry just get run over. We can kill our share on the way."

"Guess I'll let the other three know… Okay. We're gonna make the rounds. Keep an eye out for sharks."

"Yeah, we've got this area covered. Haven't encountered anything we couldn't handle yet."

Maple and Sally promised to come running if anything came

up, then galloped away. Kasumi had Haku resume its prowl, on the lookout for these sharks.

"At this rate, I'm not even going to need my new skill."

"Yeah, doesn't seem like mine will see any use today, either."

Chrome and Kasumi had used their medals to acquire new combat skills, but unless they got into a tough fight, there was no real reason to bust them out.

"I took a skill with a chance of increasing the number of items produced when crafting, so it's not really combat relevant."

"Oh, but that should help with the cost-performance issue."

"A bit. What skills did you two pick?"

"Uh...well, if we find a monster worth using it on, you'll see."

"Hmm? Heh-heh, I think we just got a bit of Maple's luck," Kasumi said.

Her eyes were on a manta ray drifting gracefully across the sky. They knew right away this was a rare monster like Maple's shark. And they weren't about to let it escape.

"Kasumi, head for it!"

"Already am!"

Kasumi had Haku speed up, slithering directly toward the manta.

The monster spotted them coming and generated a blue magic circle in its maw, unleashing a gush of water—like the one that had sent Maple flying.

"Time to show you what I've got! Watch this! Guardian!"

Chrome held his shield aloft, and the deluge swallowed the three of them—but Chrome soaked the entire blow and held steady.

"For a brief window after activation, I take less damage and protect those around me. Plus, status effects are all negated! It's like Martyr's Devotion for mortals."

The main difference was the damage reduction, which was

significant enough to make it usable even with Chrome's more reasonable VIT. Since it canceled out effects like knockback and poison, it made him even more reliable as a tank.

"Then let me show mine off, too. Armored Arms. Third Blade: Blue Moon."

When the deluge died down, Kasumi used a skill to leap high in the air, getting above the manta and slicing away at it. With the two arms floating next to her adding to the damage, the monster swayed. Still, it *was* a rare monster—and this alone did not finish off its HP.

As Kasumi started to fall, she righted herself, raising her katana once more.

"First Blade: Heat Haze!"

Even mid-fall, this skill let her move in ways that would normally be impossible. She was warped right in front of the manta and slashed at it, hurting it further—and as she fell again, she activated her newest skill.

"Specter of Carnage."

Her body began to glow with a red light.

Chrome used Taunt to pull the manta's attacks, watching Kasumi closely.

"Third Blade: Blue Moon!"

The same skill she'd used a moment before. Once more, she rose at physics-defying speeds, slashing the manta and passing up above it. Now all she needed to do was repeat the attack as she fell. Seeing how little HP it had left, Kasumi was sure she could finish it off.

"First Blade: Heat Haze!"

She teleported once more, swinging her blade to finish this before the manta could even react. Unable to endure her onslaught, the manta burst into light, leaving a lump of water behind. Kasumi

caught that with both hands, called for Haku, and righted herself just in time to land neatly on the snake's head.

"......Did you change classes to Acrobat?"

"Heh-heh, it's definitely movement only possible in a game."

"Was that your new skill, Kasumi?"

"Yes. Moving like that took some practice, though. Basically, it provides a temporary drastic cooldown reduction. The catch is that if I don't kill anything while it's active, *all* my skills go on cooldown."

"Whoa...that's a serious double-edge sword. But the sheer burst-damage potential makes up for it. No way you could dance across the sky without that."

"Exactly. If I can chain in other movement skills, I should be able to pull off some neat moves."

"Moves that defy common sense."

"Everyone's getting so good! Absolutely worth backing you up."

"Hmm. Was my pick too conservative?"

"Heh-heh, you're doing just fine, Chrome."

"Agreed."

However, Chrome didn't seem reassured.

Sally's horse was galloping across the field. Maple kept one hand tight around Sally to avoid falling off, but her other arm was transformed into a Gatling gun, courtesy of Machine God. She was unloading on every school of fish they spotted.

"Mounted target practice?"

"A hundred percent accuracy...isn't possible, but if I shoot a hundred bullets, some are bound to hit!"

"But your aim is definitely improving. As weird as that is for a shield class..."

"Heh-heh. Gotta get as good as Wilbert someday!"

"Ah-ha-ha, let's be realistic. But if you do miss any... Cyclone Cutter!" Sally's wind spell took out the few fish that slipped through. "Mm, got 'em."

"Wow!"

They were traveling at top speed, and she had one hand on the reins. Attacking like that was no easy feat. Sally had to keep one eye on the path ahead to avoid running into anything, while also scanning for anything that slipped through Maple's barrage, and she had to react instantly to clean up those monsters—then on top of all that, she was watching to see if their kills dropped anything.

"I'll take out anything you miss. Together, we can hit a hundred percent."

"You betcha!"

They galloped on awhile longer, encountering not only sharks and mantas but also octopuses and squids. All of these giant sea creatures attacked with water, with no other moves of note; they didn't pose a real threat. After fighting a few and figuring out their patterns, Sally decided they didn't even need to dismount. Maple would just start shooting, then they'd gallop out of the monsters' range. Once they reached a safe distance, Maple would keep attacking like a stationary turret until the monster was down.

"Hmm, saves us the time spent getting on and off the horse."

"Wow. You can even dodge on horseback!"

"That's just how basic their attacks are. As long as I can see 'em coming, it's easy."

After the fighting was over, they just had to hoover up any drops, then rinse and repeat. Large or small, each monster was only worth one kill, but knowing they'd always drop the materials Iz wanted was good reason to hit the big ones before other players got them.

"It's still only day one. Soon enough, the hive mind'll have figured out where they're most likely to spawn."

"Will that make it easier to farm?"

"Uh…hard to say. If everyone clusters at those spots, the competition will be stiff."

"Oh, right. In that case, we'll have to find a spot all our own!"

"That'd be ideal. Another argument in favor of running all over the map like this."

One reason they'd decided to stay on the seventh stratum was the horse—a quick means of transport that could carry them both. And this was by far the largest map, which made it easier to avoid direct competition.

But almost any player could get a horse, and Sally was not the only one who'd thought of this approach.

"Ack."

"Yo, Sally! How's it going?"

Two players approached from up ahead, each on their own horse. Frederica and Drag from the Order of the Holy Sword had come to say hello.

"We're doing all right. Keeping an eye out for a good farming spot, relaxing. You?"

"Same. We're taking out the fish and the big ones, but…"

Frederica glanced at Drag, who shrugged.

"The last event had monsters worth battling, but these are practically made of paper."

"Tissue paper."

Maple and Sally had thought the same. They knew the monsters in the last event had been intended as a challenge, and these weren't, but even by that metric, the fish were sorely lacking in HP and attack variety.

"Pretty much what we were thinking."

"Yeah, so…we're wondering if there isn't something *else* going on. We're hunting for clues."

The Order had a *lot* of members, and with their entire outfit on the prowl—if they hadn't found anything, it must be well hidden.

"Mm-hmm. Sadly, we don't know any intel worth trading yet. Honest truth."

"Tch, Frederica! This was a dead end."

"They're Sally and Maple! I figured they'd have stumbled across it first thing."

"If we do, we'll let you know! Right, Sally?"

"Yeah…in exchange for what *you've* got up your sleeve."

"I'll have something juicy ready. It'll be worth your while! Laters."

"If there is anything. Hope we get PvP soon!"

"We're raring to go!"

"Same here."

Frederica gave them a little wave and trotted after Drag. They were soon out of sight.

"Intel, huh?" Maple said. "We don't even have any *clues*."

"True. Maybe we should try a different approach."

"……? You mean, like, check other floors?"

Sally shook her head. She figured they'd learned all they could racing around the fields; they needed to try a different zone entirely.

"Dungeons. Let's take a few runs on one."

"Oh! They might have changed for the event?"

"Yep. One run might not be enough, so let's do a few."

"Then let's pick one with a short path to the boss."

"And if it feels like a bust, we go back to shark hunting. The event's only just started, so plenty of time left to figure things out."

"Agreed!"

They'd cleared a number of seventh-stratum dungeons together. They picked a shorter one and galloped toward it.

The simplest dungeon they'd found was the colosseum-style monster rush that Velvet and Hinata had taken them to.

The difficulty was determined by number of participants, and there was a set amount of fights and enemies, so they knew they could get through it easily. Ideal for checking event changes.

"Let's give it a go."

"Mm-hmm!"

Maple and Sally stepped into the dungeon, trouncing each set of statues in turn. Like they'd predicted, things *were* different. Previously, there had been no monsters in the halls among statue chambers, but this time they regularly encountered the event-limited tropical fish.

"Okay. They really do show up *everywhere*."

"They sure weren't here before!"

"Exactly. A dead giveaway. And..."

Sally took a few steps forward, passing through the school and cutting them all down.

"Yup, they're not any stronger."

"Wow, Sally. You're amazing."

"Only places we're not seeing them are the statue rooms. Probably the boss room, too."

They moved on, keeping an eye out for anything else different and cleaning up the event monsters. Soon, they were at the boss room.

As they stepped in, they found a statue with an ax in each hand—a different loadout from their previous run, where they'd had a four-player party.

"It should be weaker than last time...right?"

"According to Velvet. But whether it's a good fit for us is another question. Careful!"

They were here to investigate, so it would never do to accidentally lose. They readied their weapons and prepared for combat.

"It'll likely take big swings, so I'll slip past and hack away."

"Go for it!"

Sally sped off, and Maple deployed her artillery, firing. As Sally got close, the right ax swung down.

"No prob! Superspeed!"

Sally blurred into an evasive move, dodging sideways as the ax hit the ground and leaping through the resulting dust cloud, landing on top of the ax like she did that every day. Slashing away at the stone arm, she raced up to the statue's shoulder. Using oversize enemies' attacks against them was one of Sally's specialties, and this rush did a ton of damage. While she was at it, the statue used its other arm to throw an ax at Maple.

"Whoa!"

Maple had been focused on shooting, so she didn't dodge in time—the ax scored a direct hit. With a clang, the ax bounced off her, and Maple's damaged weapons exploded, sending her tumbling across the ground.

"......Yikes!" she said, dusting herself off. Unharmed. She tried to redeploy her weapons.

"Maple!"

"......!"

Quickly catching the reason behind Sally's yelp, Maple switched plans, blowing up the weapons to rocket herself forward. The statue tried to swat her with its left palm, but once the distance between the girls was small enough, Sally used a skill.

"Substitute!"

Sally had been on the statue's head and Maple in midair—now their positions were reversed. Sally righted herself and landed on the ground below, while Maple made her arm a tentacle and swallowed up the statue's head.

"Cool!"

The writhing tentacles sprayed black mist, grasping the head through an intense shower of red damage sparks. Sally knew her plan had worked.

Maple had taken full advantage of her new proximity with the statue. Once they swapped positions, Maple was free to slam home her highest damage skill, Devour. Any boss that let Sally get close exposed itself to an unpreventable point-to-point substitution that put Maple right on top of them.

Maple's tentacles crushed the statue's head, and as the last of the red sparks faded, the entire statue burst into a shower of light.

Sally caught Maple as she fell and set her gently on the ground.

"Well done."

"Yeah! That worked like a charm!"

"......And there *was* a difference."

"......?"

Maple gave her a puzzled look, having noticed nothing amiss. Sally pointed at the ground around them. There were several puddles—and not ones Sally's skills had generated.

"It didn't drop any materials or behave any different, but if there's water left behind, this must have *something* to do with the ninth event."

The statue itself had made no water-based attacks, but in light of this event's theme, odds were high there was something event-related going on here—something *other* than the event monsters.

"Okay. Let's try fighting it again! Maybe we'll get some good drops."

"Yeah. It wasn't that strong, so let's hit it again."

They hopped on the magic circle and immediately headed back in.

CHAPTER 2

Defense Build and the War Hammers

While Maple and Sally were running a seventh-layer dungeon, Mai and Yui were hunting event monsters on the fifth stratum. They'd chosen that over the current map because the field was brightly lit, and most monsters were cloud-based and slow-moving. They could focus on event monsters with far less risk of ambush. At their level, they were still getting a decent amount of XP, too.

If Maple and Sally weren't sweating these foes, that meant the all-attack twins could do their thing and one-shot every event monster they saw.

Even on the front lines of the seventh stratum, the only enemies that could survive their hits were bosses.

Tsukimi and Yukimi had increased their movement speed, so they were running around the map—and had just encountered a shark.

"Look! That one's rare!"

"Yeah…! Let's take it out!"

They had their bears go separate ways to avoid an unfortunate party wipe.

"Farshot!"

Yui swung her hammer, firing a shock wave that rocketed toward the shark. But it swam through the air out of the attack's range, then fired a torrent of water at Mai as she closed in.

"Titan's Lot!"

Rather than take evasive actions, Mai raised both her hammers and swung them hard. They hit the water, generating a white light—and deflecting the water right back at the shark.

"Nice, Mai! Yukimi!"

Yui had her bear run up, positioning her where she could slam her hammers against the underside of the flinching shark. That alone did enough damage to make the shark literally explode.

"Yes! That was perfect timing, Mai."

"Was it...? Good!"

This was the new skill the twins had spent their medals on. If their STR was greater than the damage of an incoming attack, the skill would negate and reflect that damage. With no defense to speak of, they risked taking lots of damage—but their attack was usually stronger. It wasn't a guaranteed counter, but it played to their strengths, and when they were out of other options, it never hurt to try. If they managed to defeat their foes' best attacks, they could turn the whole fight around instantly.

Most of the time, they were focused on using their bears' movement speed to evade. But if an attack was definitely going to hit, this gave them a chance to retaliate.

By this point, they'd already confirmed that none of the event monsters on the fifth floor could match their STR. As long as they reacted in time, they could knock any attack back.

They picked up the drop and leaned against a nearby cloud wall, taking a break.

"I was so nervous when we picked it out. I'm glad it's actually working."

"Yeah! With our attack power, it should prove pretty useful!"

If anyone else used it, this skill didn't do much besides offering a minor chance of surprising a foe. But for Mai and Yui, it was something that could turn a boss's best moves against it.

"We'll have to figure out what to do with the next medals!"

Since Maple Tree kept posting top results, they were getting a steady stream of medals that could be exchanged for skills or items. The twins were already considering what type of skill to get next.

"Yeah...there's so many good ones."

"I know! But I was thinking..."

"Hmm? What?"

Yui took a moment to collect her thoughts. So far, both twins had picked the same skills every time. There were benefits to matching up, and given their identical builds, they were both in the market for similar skill effects. So far, every choice they'd made had been the best option to improve themselves.

"We almost always fight together, so I thought it might be fun if we could find some skills that let us play off each other."

At this point, they were both plenty powerful. In the prelims of the last event, they'd done quite well and gained some confidence.

"Yeah, that could be fun. And it might surprise people."

When they'd gone up against Dread in the fourth event, they'd worked together. Since each sister knew how the other fought, skills that strengthened their teamwork might take them places.

"In that case...I'd like to back up your attacks, Yui."

"Then I'll get better attacks!"

Working together, only one of them actually needed to hit. Now they just had to find the right skills for this new strategy.

"Sally always does it, so I'm already looking at the skills."

"Heh-heh, but we won't have the medals for a while yet."

"We can always scour the map for them, so… Hmm, maybe we should focus on that."

"And then…ha-ha, I bet we end up both taking the same skills again."

If they did that, then either one of them could start the combo. Best to spend their medals on hidden tricks their foes wouldn't see coming.

"Then let's go find more monsters!"

"Good idea."

"Aiiiiieeee!"

""?!""

As they started to stand, they heard a scream from above. Their heads snapped up, and they saw someone falling from high above. They had their bears rush over, trying to catch her. But the falling girl stopped upside down right before impact, hovering as if gravity did not exist. A second girl came wafting down after her.

"Whew! That was way too close!"

"Always make sure you're on solid ground…"

The girls hovering before them were Velvet and Hinata. The latter's gravity skill had saved Velvet from an untimely death. When Velvet noticed Mai and Yui had their arms outstretched to catch her, her face lit up. She waved at them and asked Hinata to set her down.

"Whoops," she said, looking a bit sheepish. "That must have been, like, a huge shock! My bad!"

"No problem at all! Um, aren't you…Velvet?"

"Hmm? That's my name, but… Oh, you're part of Maple Tree! She tell you 'bout me?"

"Yes!"

Mai and Yui were thrilled by this chance encounter. They'd

had a question on their minds ever since they first heard about Thunder Storm's antics.

Maple's stories made it sound like Velvet's and Hinata's skills played off each other. The twins had just been thinking about trying to add more teamwork and were looking for new ideas. Maple and Sally also had amazing combos, but all of theirs were based on the kind of powerhouse stuff nobody else could really imitate—it wasn't especially helpful.

The twins explained what they'd been talking about, and Velvet started nodding.

"Aha! Teamwork is great!"

"Mostly…you should focus on what you're best at."

"Exactly! With us, Hinata locks 'em all down, and I take it from there."

"So…you each have a role to play?"

"Um…I think that makes it easier."

That did make sense. Maybe the twins should choose different skills after all.

"But that's us, not you!" Velvet said. "I bet there's a totally different strategy that'll make you kick all kinds of ass!"

This pair from Thunder Storm had weapons and fighting styles that were polar opposites. With the twins, everything was identical—and that let them take a different approach.

"Hmm, this is so hard!"

"I know, Mai."

"Okay, then—why not, like, have a look at how we fight? Maybe that'll provide some inspiration!"

In exchange, Velvet only asked for a look at how Mai and Yui fought. They shook on that deal.

"And we can share a damn good way to rack up event kills! As thanks for, like, trying to catch me."

"Are you sure?"

"We already got heaps of materials. There's a bit of a trick to it, but this is a co-op event, so it's the sort of thing you *want* to share, y'know?"

"That...makes sense."

The twins were surprised by how many drops Thunder Storm had already gathered. Mai and Yui agreed to these terms, and the four of them headed off to a nearby location where they could quickly rack up kills.

Tsukimi and Yukimi were bounding across the clouds. Velvet and Hinata were hitching a ride, negating their natural speed discrepancy.

"Mm-hmm! These are rad."

Letting the wind whip her hair, Velvet stroked Tsukimi's fur.

"What kind of monster did you tame, Velvet?"

"Me? Heh-heh-heh—that's definitely top secret!"

"The other guild members made us swear not to tell. Sorry."

Sally had already informed the twins that no one had seen Thunder Storm's pets. They'd just been curious, so they didn't press the point further.

"Nobody's seen them yet?"

"Not that I know of!" Velvet declared.

Mai and Yui had seen all of Maple Tree's pets and knew just how powerful they could be. Most had multiple skills, and keeping those under wraps was a big advantage—it made total sense that some guilds would maintain a veil of secrecy until the next big PvP event.

"Oh, almost there! Never been on a bear before; that was so damn fun!"

Before them, a large hole opened in the clouds below.

This was Velvet's destination. The twins peered over the edge and saw platforms jutting out of the white cloud walls. It looked like they'd need to bound down those to reach the bottom.

But there were also monsters on the way; they spotted several black thunderclouds and schools of fish from the event.

"There's a dungeon at the bottom!"

They would have to be very careful on the way down. Mai and Yui put their game faces on. These platforms made for dangerous footing, and there were a *lot* of monsters around.

"Here we go! Hinata, hit us."

"On it. Gravity Control."

Hinata's skill instantly wrapped all four of them in a black shroud, and their feet lifted off the ground.

"We can float as long as the skill is active. We can't move that fast, though."

The twins were pulled out over the shaft with Velvet and Hinata. At the center, they heard a cry from one side.

"Let's light this place up! Thunder God Advent! Eye of the Storm! Lightning Rain! Thunderbolt Alley!"

Velvet fired up a series of skills that filled the air with electricity. Any foes that stepped in range would be fried to a crisp.

"Here we go!" she yelled, dead center over the shaft—and electrified the entire circumference of the pit.

Now they merely had to slowly descend through it.

"Super effective! Oh, but don't, like, fret. This ain't all I got."

She shot the twins a grin, perfectly aware nobody else could fight like this.

"Can we really...learn anything here?"

"I'm less and less confident."

As they watched the lightning storm mercilessly slaughter any and all monsters, Hinata took them slowly down the shaft.

This would likely be a bracing challenge done right, but thanks to Velvet, no actual fighting proved necessary. They were at the base in mere minutes.

When the storm stopped, they gathered up everything the zapped monsters had dropped and turned toward the side passage leading into the dungeon.

"That got us a decent haul, huh? Normally we just, like, jump down."

No matter how fast they fell, Hinata's gravity skills could catch them before they hit the bottom. Going at that speed, anything that resisted lightning would survive their descent, but since the goal this time was the easily killed event fish, that wasn't an issue.

This certainly explained why their teamwork let them quickly rack up their event kill count.

"We looked far and wide for a place we could rack up kills fast! This pit is the best spot around!"

They'd been waiting for the respawn and then had dropped down again, but this time they headed farther in. The goal—to see how Mai and Yui fought. There was also a fairly efficient farming area inside, and that's where they were headed—and not the boss room.

"Oh, but we ain't that good at protection. You gotta watch yourselves!"

"Nobody else can do...what Maple does."

""We know!""

Velvet and Hinata were both built for offense, not defense. Neither of them had skills like Cover or Martyr's Devotion that could be used to absorb a blow for someone else.

They headed down the cloud corridors, navigating several forks and going past the odd group of monsters. Given the layout, the trash mobs were easily handled by Velvet's hallway-filling lightning bolts or the twins' Farshot attacks. Nothing could dodge those, and they turned to cinders on sight. No special teamwork or combos necessary.

This went on for a while, but eventually, a bulky foe moved into sight around the corner.

"Oh! A marlin! Hinata!"

"I'm on it. Gravity Shackles. Thought Freeze."

At her cry, black chains shot out of the floor, binding the marlin, and a blast of chilly air immobilized it completely. While it was unable to fight back, Velvet charged in, wreathed in lightning, and slid underneath the giant fish.

"Double Whammy! Thunderclap!"

A heavy lightning-charged two-hit combo pounded the marlin, sparks flying. Then the ground around Velvet lit up, and a huge column of lightning generated around her, blowing the marlin away.

"Whew. Nice one, Hinata!"

"That went well."

The twins gaped. That marlin had been vaporized in an instant, unable to take any action. Hinata's and Velvet's moves worked in perfect tandem.

"So, what'd ya think?"

"You were amazing! So smooth!"

"Aw, you're making me blush. The secret to teamwork is, like, having a plan and sticking to it."

It would've been impossible for the combo to have gone that smoothly without extensive planning. Velvet and Hinata had come up with strategies that worked against players and different types of monsters, then practiced them over and over.

That polish made everything super quick, from start to finish.

"The marlins can null damage-dealing skills, so we've gotta have Hinata lock 'em down right away."

"Otherwise...I'm only helpful at the monster house we're headed for."

"We need plans..."

"Hmm..."

Watching them fight firsthand left the twins hung up on

the same thing. They both had the same role, so their teamwork wouldn't work the same way.

"A dedicated support player's great. Hinata can work with other attackers—doesn't have to be *me*."

That said, Hinata insisted she couldn't work well with just *anyone*. Still, the obvious conclusion here was that support skills were worth having.

Their thoughts going in circles, Mai and Yui headed farther into the dungeon, watching Thunder Storm's teamwork as they went. In time, the party reached their destination—a space as big as any boss room.

"Head right to the center!"

""Okay!""

Once they'd made it there, the floor changed colors, and monsters spawned all around.

"This trap, like, floods us with monsters! Including event ones!"

Since this monster trap spawned so many monsters, while the event was active, it also spawned fish. If you could actually survive that onslaught, stepping on this trap was a lot more efficient than roaming the map.

"Cocytus!"

Before the spawns even completed, before any monsters could act—Hinata froze the entire area.

"Hit 'em hard!"

""Okay!""

Between the lightning and the one-shot kill hammers, this was a killzone. There was never a chance the thaw would come in time.

When the fight was over, they exited the dungeon to go their separate ways.

"I hope we, like, taught you something today."

"Remember, you can't fight like us...you have to find your own way."

"Right!"

"Thank you!"

"I hope you get damn good! Can't wait to fight you!"

Velvet wasn't just being nice. If the twins improved, that would be one more thing to look forward to in the inevitable PvP event.

The twins waved them off, then looked at each other.

"......What now?"

"Um...one of us takes a support skill?"

"One that plays to our strengths..."

"Ours alone..."

""..........!""

They closed their eyes, thinking; then an idea struck them both. Their eyes opened, they fired off a message, and then set off for the guild home.

When they arrived, they found Maple waiting for them—like they'd requested. She and Sally had still been doing back-to-back runs of the statue dungeon when the twins' message arrived, so they'd packed it up and headed to the fifth-stratum guild home.

"Oh, they're here! Any luck?"

"Yes! The fifth stratum has good visibility, so we can fight safely."

"And we just ran a dungeon with Velvet and Hinata."

"You did? That's a first!" Sally said.

Mai and Yui launched into the full story, including how they were effectively grinding kills for the event.

"Interesting... I bet we could replicate that. Maple can handle the falling and the monster house. Definitely more efficient than roaming the map. Hadn't occurred to me."

"Then let's go fight some monsters!"

"Actually, there was something else we wanted to talk about."

Their message had just asked for Maple's help, so she'd assumed they needed the protection of Martyr's Devotion.

"Here's the thing…"

Mai began explaining what they were trying to do. When they were done, Maple was nodding.

"Mm-hmm! Okay! I'm in!"

"……Sorry, nothing I can do there. Maple, this one's all you."

Sally put her hands together. She'd have to go back to monster farming.

"Yep, good luck killing those monsters!"

"Thanks. Hope to hear good things from all of you."

""Same!""

With their goals aligned, the three girls set out.

Their destination: the sixth stratum. Supposedly, the event monster spawn rate was set pretty low there, and there were no fish at all—so not many players were around. There were lots of ghosts instead, which was why Sally wasn't helping.

"Here?"

"Should be!"

If the event monsters didn't spawn often, then that was a sign it really wasn't part of the event at all.

"Events like this, it's totally fine to just do other things!"

Maple had attained a whole new form during such an event before. There was no reason to limit yourself.

"Now we just gotta do the same as before. Um…"

Maple put a hand to her mouth, remembering what she'd done.

"Yeah, let's just give it a shot! If it doesn't work, we can do better next time!"

""Thanks again!""

"If it helps you two get stronger, I'm happy to help! Let's get those Helping Hands!"

Maple threw out a fist, and the twins bumped it.

Yes—the goal today was to get Mai and Yui what Maple had found here before—the Helping Hands.

After seeing how Thunder Storm fought, Mai and Yui had considered their own strengths and reached the same conclusion. Making sure their hits landed didn't require more skills, and they didn't need to increase their poor mobility—they just needed *more hammers.* Their accuracy had dramatically improved when they switched to two, and the same thing would happen if they had *four.*

"First, uh…kill a lot of ghosts here, and if a blue one shows up, follow it!"

"Got it!"

"Make sure we exorcise them!"

"Huh…?"

Mai didn't know how to do that. Mai and Yui had never really used items to tackle enemies one at a time. Swinging their hammers took care of any monster, no matter how much it tried to reduce their damage. They were barely aware the game had items and charms specifically designed for dealing with the undead.

Maple filled them in and handed over some of her extras. She'd bought a lot, but their uses were limited, so she had plenty left over.

"Last time, the blue ghost showed up after I exorcised everything on this mountain. I think that's the key monster!"

"Everything?"

It had taken Maple quite a while, so the twins settled in for the long haul.

"But this time there's three of us! Way better!"

"Meaning?"

"Just you wait!"

Maple found an open area, called Syrup out, made him giant, and used her favorite turtle-back skill.

"Heaven's Throne!"

This skill—and Martyr's Devotion—made the twins and the ground around them glow. As long as they were bathed in that light, they were impervious to all harm.

"With my throne out, the ghosts can't do anything. But solo, I can't exorcise them and use it at the same time."

"That's why three's better!"

Giant Syrup couldn't move around much in this forest. Last time, she'd used the throne but had been forced to wait for the cooldown every time she put it away. If she left all exorcism duties to Mai and Yui, all she had to do was provide the advantageous domain, and they'd make much better progress.

"I'll be flying around up above the trees, so lemme know when you're ready to move on!"

""Gotcha!""

"Okay! Let's get this party started!"

Their plan settled, they made swift progress on these exorcisms— they had twice the exorcisers. Maple's anti-evil field was quite large, and the twins' bears made them much more agile, so they could dart around the zone, taking out ghosts quickly.

They roamed the mountain for a while, riding Tsukimi and Yukimi. In time, the throngs of ghosts died out, and they spotted the blue ghost Maple had mentioned.

"Mai, is that it?"

"Hmm…let's have Maple check."

They called her down, and once she was sure the area was ghost-free, she got off her throne and jumped down from her turtle.

"Hokay! Uh, where is it?"

"Right there!"

"Yup! That's it! Now we just gotta follow it around."

Maple knew there was more fighting ahead, so she left Syrup flying around above them and hopped on Yukimi's back for the ghost pursuit.

Like Maple's previous run, they soon found themselves before a cross on the mountain peak. They got ready and waited.

""Whoa?!""

"Here we go!"

As they stood before the cross, hands reached up and grabbed the girls, dragging them down to the darkness below.

Flung forcibly into the combat zone, they witnessed a giant red ghost appear before them. It was the same one Maple had met while exploring the sixth stratum originally, its upper half leaning out of a rift in the darkness, long arms dangling.

"It was a tough fight solo, but with you two around, we've got this! Inspire! Syrup, Red Garden."

Maple jumped up on Syrup and sat down on her throne, sealing the ghost's skills. She also buffed the twins' damage. Now they were ready.

""Destroy Mode!""

They'd known this fight was coming, so before they stepped inside, the twins had used a ton of Doping Seeds to bump their STR as high as it would go. This skill was the final touch. They were also using items to grant their hammers the fire element. As the boss approached, they raised their burning hammers high.

"Go!"

""Double Impact!""

Two hammers from each twin slammed the reaching arms. So many damage sparks sprayed, it almost seemed like the ghost's red body was exploding.

Maple had managed to chip away at it with charms and salt—and the fact that she'd pulled that off proved it had a relatively small HP pool. Could a monster like that survive a full-power pounding from the twins?

The damage-spark spray gave way to an even brighter light—the boss that had given Maple so much trouble, downed in a single attack.

"Wow! You two are so strong!"

"It worked!"

"Yes…thank goodness!"

As they celebrated, a magic circle appeared nearby.

"Huh?"

"What's wrong?"

"Um, last time this place turned white, and I got a pendant…"

But this time, only the exit appeared.

This left them unable to get the equipment they were after. Maple started humming and hawing, trying to figure out why things had turned out different.

"Um, last time the fight lasted ages, and I used tons of skills… and charms…"

"Maybe that's it. You've gotta beat the boss the right way!"

They'd used a lot of charms to beat all those ghosts, so it made sense they'd have to beat the boss with those, too.

"Oh…maybe you're right!"

"So we've gotta leave enough HP to finish it off with the charms."

"Ugh, I hope we get it next time…"

Their first run, they'd gone all out and pulverized the boss, so now they'd have to make adjustments and leave the boss's HP in the red. The twins were probably the only people who would ever run into this problem, but it was a pretty major one.

In later phases, they'd lose track of where their party members were. And this boss had attacks that even worked on Maple. There was a very real chance that if they weren't careful, the boss could take them all down.

But they soon made up their minds.

"We've got time! Let's just keep trying. Even if we accidentally beat it, that just means we're still alive!"

""True!""

The three of them began experimenting, trying to find a way to *not quite* kill the boss.

After several attempts, they managed to reduce their buffs the perfect amount and successfully leave the boss hanging on by a handful of HP.

"Ready! Let's do this!"

""Yeah!""

Before the boss could act again, Mai and Yui started slapping charms on it. That proved enough to empty the HP bar, and it vanished. Their first success—and they waited with bated breath. The darkness around crumbled away, and they found themselves in the white space Maple had described.

"Woo! We did it!"

Delighted by their first success, Maple ran over to the cross.

The scene she'd witnessed when she first got Helping Hands played out, and as party leader, Maple found herself with the pendant around her neck.

She took it off, checking the name.

"Let's see…cool, it's the same accessory!"

Then she held it out to the twins.

"You first, Yui."

"You're sure, Mai?"

"Mm-hmm. Heh-heh! You look so eager."

Yui wasn't about to argue. She quickly equipped it.

"Um…okay! Now some weapons…"

Yui equipped weapons to the arms floating beside her, gaining an extra hammer per arm.

Two big crystal hammers floated on either side of her. She tried moving them around.

"Whoa, this is hard!"

"Yeah, I'm still not good at precision stuff or moving them while I'm doing anything else."

But the twins didn't *need* precision. They could just fling the hammers wildly about, and if they made contact—the battle was over.

"Okay, let's get Mai's! ……?"

"Yes! ……What's wrong?" Mai asked.

Maple looked like she'd just realized something obvious.

"Um, so last time I really struggled, and I figured I'd never come back, so I didn't really think this through. But what if…?"

Maple offered a suggestion, and they both started nodding.

"Cool! Then let's get right on that! We've got a lot of fighting ahead of us!"

""Yeah!""

Once more, the three of them ventured into the boss room.

A few days passed.

Iz was spending time in her workshop, making one of each item she could craft from the event monster drops.

"Whew, that should do it. The rare drops sure do make a lot of stuff for underwater exploration. I guess that makes sense, but…is that gonna be important on the next stratum?"

If they'd added all this stuff, Iz assumed there'd be a use for it. But this was all just speculation for now, so even if all the items did was help scour the existing oceans and lakes, swell.

"I guess I'll be leaving the fighting to the others…"

She sat down to take a break—and heard voices through the door.

""""Iz!"""""

Maple, Mai, and Yui all came in. They'd clearly been running, and Iz instantly knew they wanted her to make them something.

"Wh-what's the rush?"

"We need weapons for the twins!"

"Weapons? Did they break? I just did maintenance, so I assumed they'd be good for a while…but obviously I'm happy to."

"Thank you!"

"Um, so Yui and I each need six hammers."

"S-six?! Each?!"

She'd assumed they'd fought a weapon-wrecking monster, but this request was clearly of an entirely different nature.

"H-hold on, I'm lost…"

Realizing they'd skipped the most important part, they explained.

"Um…easier if we just show you," Maple said.

She glanced at Mai and Yui, who changed up their gear. A moment later, six white hands floated around each of them.

That was enough for Iz to work it out.

Players could equip *three* accessories. That meant they could replace their STR-buff equipment with more copies of Helping Hands, each allowing two additional weapons. They'd have to switch back to use their pet bears, but this allowed them *eight* hammers of instant death they could have only dreamed of before.

"My mind's caught up…still a bit dizzy…but sure! Twelve hammers, all top quality, coming right up!"

""Thank you so much!""

"Once they're ready, we'll have to try them out!"

""Exactly!""

Iz alone wondered what other players would make of *that*.

---

335 Name: Anonymous Greatsworder
Doing my bit in this event, but it's nice you don't have to be that intense about it.

336 Name: Anonymous Archer
We know what stratums are best yet?

337 Name: Anonymous Spear Master
Less about which floor than where on the floor.
Every layer's got spots with better spawn rates or where you can kill 'em easier.

338 Name: Anonymous Archer
Since I'm all ranged, I'm mostly fighting where I can't get surrounded. Not too efficient.

339 Name: Anonymous Greatsworder
But since we're all hitting the goal together, minor stuff like that won't matter.

340 Name: Anonymous Mage
Yo.

341 Name: Anonymous Spear Master
That so ominous.

342 Name: Anonymous Greatsworder
Word.

343 Name: Anonymous Archer
That's the "Yo" that precedes an *anecdote*.

344 Name: Anonymous Mage
I saw the damnedest thing.

345 Name: Anonymous Spear Master
An event monster?
Or a player that's *like* a monster?

346 Name: Anonymous Mage
The latter.

347 Name: Anonymous Archer
Does their name start with *M*?

348 Name: Anonymous Mage
Technically. One of them.

349 Name: Anonymous Greatsworder
?????

350 Name: Anonymous Mage
Long story short.
Mai and Yui are now octo-wielding hammers.

351 Name: Anonymous Greatsworder
?????????????????????

352 Name: Anonymous Archer
That doesn't make any sense.

353 Name: Anonymous Great Shielder
News to me! Nobody tells me anything!
I've just been out diligently grinding!
I'll have to go look... I bet Maple was involved...

354 Name: Anonymous Spear Master
Did all these fish provoke a growth spurt?! Too much XP?!

355 Name: Anonymous Greatsworder
Leveling up doesn't increase your weapon slots! Or does it?!

356 Name: Anonymous Mage
From a distance, I saw white and black forms wheeling through the air, and when I got closer, they were *humans*.

357 Name: Anonymous Spear Master
That's just unnecessary DPS.
For what enemy? They'd liquify anything with that loadout!

358 Name: Anonymous Great Shielder
They grow up so fast... They're all amazing...

359 Name: Anonymous Greatsworder
I pity the bosses.

360 Name: Anonymous Archer
Well, if they dodge...

361 Name: Anonymous Great Shielder
The hitboxes alone are brutal.
I ain't seen it myself, so I dunno the trick, but with the size of their hammers, if they even graze you, it's fatal.
And they got eight? Get out.

362 Name: Anonymous Mage
Eight hammers all spinning through the air.
Monsters shattering.

363 Name: Anonymous Spear Master
Status effect: brain melting.

364 Name: Anonymous Archer
Not really spinning...
More like a jackhammer of death.

365 Name: Anonymous Great Shielder
Our primary offense crew sure does come through!

366 Name: Anonymous Greatsworder
They already were!
Dear...lord...

CHAPTER 3

Defense Build and a Boss Rush

Mai and Yui were back on the fifth floor, fighting event monsters and practicing their octo-wield technique. Maple had just filled in Sally on how this came to pass.

"Uh-huh. Well, that does seem like it would work for them. But if someone else asks what they'd need it for, I'm kind of at a loss."

With the twins' stats, this was a totally different thing than Sally or Kasumi upping their weapon count. Neither twin needed to be all that precise, so the difficulty of controlling the extra weapons didn't really matter. The six extra hammers offered only benefits.

"At this point, we don't really need to worry about our party having enough offense. They've got more weapons, and I bet their STR keeps leaping upward, too."

Thus far, Mai's and Yui's insane burst damage had largely been their final weapon against bosses, and this was definitely the logical extreme of that play style.

"And if we're talking party play, we'll wanna strengthen our options against anyone the twins will struggle with."

"Mm-hmm."

"Like, any opponent so fast, the girls can't get in range."

Sally threw out a few suggestions—all offense-based. Defensively, Maple already had the twins covered. Martyr's Devotion and Heaven's Throne completely negated Mai's and Yui's low defense. And functionally speaking, this was so ridiculously good, there was no need to try and improve it.

"You always played off one another well, but now all three of you are so good, it's hard to find ways to make that better."

In Sally's mind, if they ever had to split into teams for PvP, having these three play together would be ideal.

"So we should practice our teamwork?"

"Build a repertoire of stuff you can do on the fly."

"Like you always do!"

"I'm an old hand at VR. Got lots of experience to draw on."

Sally's AGI certainly helped, but her reflexes were also much snappier than Maple's. The difference lay in something more fundamental than their stats might suggest.

"Heh-heh, wanna practice teamwork with me, too?"

"Sure! Just don't expect too much."

"Don't overthink it. Fundamentally, you're just protecting me from hits I can't afford to take, and I'm pulling aggro on anything that could hurt you."

"And that's our path to the no-damage life!"

"Exactly. You've got strong attacks of your own, so you can switch to offense when needed. For defense, we just need to trust each other."

"Right!"

Sally trusted Maple's VIT, and Maple trusted Sally's evasion. That was the foundation of their teamwork. In a close fight, that strength would pave the way to victory.

"So on that note, wanna hit up a dungeon after this?"

"Right into the teamwork practice! I'm down!"

"I knew you'd say that."

With that goal in mind, they headed where the best monsters were—the seventh stratum. They'd explored it pretty extensively, but there was still plenty left to see.

As always, Maple was on the back of Sally's horse.

"Where to this time?"

"I stumbled across a place while the three of you were busy on the sixth layer. I poked my nose inside, but it seemed hard to solo, so I turned back."

If Sally deemed it a threat, it must be a tough dungeon indeed. Maple braced herself.

"Any intel out there?"

"Not that I could find. Either it's undiscovered or deliberately kept secret. Once word gets out, I bet everyone'll be talking about it."

"...?"

"You'll see when we get there."

Through a forest, across a wasteland, over a mountain—and at last they reached a ravine.

They peered over the edge and saw steep rock walls studded with caves and stone bridges connecting the entrances. The cries of vicious-looking bird monsters echoed in the gorge; clearly, they would not let you move about in peace. Even Maple could tell the intended route would take you back and forth across this chasm.

"So we gotta head to the bottom?"

"Yep. And to get there..."

"We jump!"

"Exactly. Shortcut!"

No need to take a slow Syrup ride. If they wanted to reach the bottom, they just needed to keep Sally in range of Martyr's Devotion and drop down together. No monster could catch a player in free fall.

"That said, I did try out one way of getting straight to the bottom on my own."

"Right, you've got your platforms and webs."

Sally had a lot of options for midair movement; even if that didn't get her all the way down, with this many rocks and bridges, she could easily make the descent while fending off the occasional monster attack.

"While I'm sure that would work out... Maple, c'mere a sec."

"Hmm? What, what?"

Sally pointed—at a place teeming with bird monsters and even more bridges. There was some height discrepancy, but done right, even a flightless player could probably take a shortcut.

"Meet the conditions, and a gate opens down there."

"A gate?!"

"Seen from directly above, those bridges form a ring."

"Oh!"

According to Sally, using basic spells of all elements would activate the transfer.

"Whoa! How'd you figure that out?"

"There were so many monsters and no solid footholds, so I figured it would be a good spot to practice evading while fending them off. Then I lucked into it."

Maple had no means of imitating that, so she was just impressed.

"That's where we're going."

"Got it!"

Maple fired up Martyr's Devotion, pulled Sally in close, and prepared to jump.

"Ready?"

"Yup!"

""Two, one!""

Both flung themselves out into the air, plummeting straight toward the valley below.

"Okay, here goes!"

"Yeah!"

Sally started flinging spells, rotating through the elements. A white light appeared at the center of the ring, wrapping around them and teleporting them away.

On the other side, the speed of the fall went away—and they found themselves on solid ground.

They were at the center of a circular space, with evenly spaced corridors leading out in every direction. As Maple looked around, the last remnant of the light that brought them here started running off across the ground—indicating a specific exit.

"Oh, is that the right way?"

"No, that just leads to the escape circle."

"Huh? We can leave right now?"

"Yep. They made it so you can bail real quick... Incoming!"

At Sally's cry, all manner of monsters came flooding in from every other corridor. Some familiar, some less so—event monsters included, no real pattern at all.

"Let's start killing!"

"Gotcha!"

This was as far as Sally's knowledge took them. Crowd control wasn't her specialty, so after one look at their numbers and the terrain, she made a strategic retreat. It didn't take her long to realize she needed Maple to get through this place.

"Focus on anything that looks pierce-y!"

"Got it! Full Deploy!"

Since there was one monster-free corridor, they kept it at their backs for some small measure of safety; then Maple started firing dead ahead. If the monsters survived that and looked dangerous, Sally ran up and slashed 'em down.

"Oboro, Whet Wisp! Spreading Flames! Water Cowl! Double Slash!"

Sally had Oboro use skills that left her wreathed in flames and made those fires spread among monsters she attacked. Then she used a skill Water Wielding had given her, adding an extra water-element hit to her attacks.

Including Chaser Blade, that meant three extra hits every time her attack connected. Each might not do that much damage, but with two daggers, she could rack up a quick combo that couldn't be ignored. Even Double Slash, ordinarily just a two-hit combo, doubled by dual-wielding alone, so she wound up doing sixteen total hits. The damage was far greater than what the skill originally offered.

"Keep it up! Predators! Hydra! Saturating Chaos!"

While Sally was stabbing one monster at a time, Maple was throwing out ranged damage skills a good distance from where Sally fought. That left the monsters running on fumes. Normally, the player stuck out in the open would be beset from all sides, but before they reached Maple, they were hit by a storm of bullets or torn up by her high-damage skills—and then they had to get past Sally. Two monsters in a row. Nothing could endure Maple's barrage long enough to take out Sally, and nothing could take Sally out fast enough to get to Maple.

Their strengths demanded more than these mobs could counter with sheer numbers.

They faced an army of slimes, orcs, goblins, and other common foes, but the parade of monsters was steadily dying down. When Sally decapitated the last of them, silence fell upon the room.

"That was a lot!"

"There were event monsters mixed in, so let's make sure we collect the drops."

As they picked up the last item, the ground began shaking, so they kept their distance and avoided the corridors. Even if those would take them somewhere, if they were still spitting out monsters, that was risky. A few moments later, another massive wave of monsters came at them.

"Again? Okay, same as the first!"

"Yeah, not ready to give up yet."

They took out this next wave just as easily, as if proving they could handle any number of attacks. Their momentum never stalled, and the number of foes steadily diminished. As the pressure on Sally eased, she started looking for any patterns here. This wave wasn't exactly the same lineup as the first, but they were still all monsters found just about anywhere.

The second wave of enemies had only proved that none of them was capable of touching Maple. Even those with piercing skills—if they couldn't get in range to use them, they might as well not have them at all.

This fight had been virtually a replay of the first, and they'd blown the horde away. The final straggler goblin emerged from the hall to find Sally waiting for it with a combo primed. It never even got its sword up.

"Whew, so much for round two."

"I'm up for more!"

"Mm, good. Without Martyr's Devotion and your barrage to thin their numbers, this wouldn't be such a breeze."

Sally could land fatal blows only on targets that were in dagger range. The reason she'd retreated the first time she'd found this place? Given the sheer numbers, breaking through their lines to tackle enemies casting spells at the back would have been a tall order when she was alone.

But between Sally's evasion and Maple's defense, that wasn't a concern.

"If it's just gonna keep throwing hordes at us, it's pretty great for hitting the event's kill quota."

"There were so many of them!"

"But if it doesn't change things up, we'll have to try heading down a corridor, even if there are monsters in it."

"Got it. I'll keep you safe when we do!"

"Yes please."

They waited a bit to see if there were more, and a tremor signaled what they'd been anticipating. This wave's monsters were clearly much more inorganic—lots of machines and golems. Something had changed. Sally soon figured out the pattern.

"One wave from each stratum…?"

"Oh! Maybe!"

Sally was hoping she was wrong. The first two waves had been creatures from the original and second stratums, and this was clearly the third. They'd definitely seen a ton of monsters like this on the third stratum. It had been a dramatic change in terrain and enemy types, which made it much easier to spot.

But if this pattern continued…there'd be one from the sixth stratum.

"For now, focus on this wave! They're already attacking!"

"Okay. Here's hoping I'm wrong…"

Worrying about the future wouldn't help with this fight. Masses of golems and machines were slowly lurching toward them.

"Commence Assault!"

Maple started firing, but the golems stepped out in front,

shielding the machines from her barrage. Frustratingly, her bullets couldn't hurt them—their HP bars refused to budge.

"Urgh, I hate golems!"

"They aren't hurting us, either, so I guess we'll have to go one at a time."

The machines were shooting right back, but just as Maple's bullets bounced off the golems, the machine soldier's bullets bounced off Maple and Sally. The golem and machines were doing well, but any ordinary monsters mixed in this crowd or machines flying too high for the golems to cover were already going down.

"Same as always, leave the tanky ones to me! Defense Break!"

Maple had yet to acquire a piercing skill. She needed to partner with a DPS player who covered that weakness. Arguably your standard offensive/defensive pairing.

"Then…how about this?"

Sally slipped through the monstrous defensive line, attacking the machines directly. If the golems tried to intervene, that exposed the machines to Maple's barrage, and if they did nothing, Sally would cut them up herself.

And the golems had no way of doing anything to Sally while she was in range of Martyr's Devotion.

The golems and Maple were both tanky, but Maple was clearly tankier.

"Rapids!"

Sally dove between the monsters as the skill activated, firing a torrent of water. This didn't do damage, but it pushed the monsters away, messing up their formation. Maple quickly laid into the exposed machines, and one after another, they burst into light.

"Defense Break! Triple Slash!"

This left them able to handle the rest in stride. For the third straight time, Maple and Sally prevailed against the enemy numbers.

When they finished off the last one, they traded high fives—and the ground shook again.

"A-already?"

"That was way faster."

They peered at the corridors, and who should appear but Maple's old nemesis.

"Ah! The Machine God!"

"Huh?! S-seriously?!"

It was a palette swap, so likely just designed to be functionally similar, but it was also clearly the first boss of this rush.

The rest of the passages were occupied by machines firing lasers just like Maple's, their sights set on our heroines.

"Okay, from here on, it won't just be trash mobs; we'll have to deal with bosses, too."

This dungeon was way harder than Sally had imagined, but she was still grinning—because she got to fight these with Maple at her side.

"Right, we've made it this far; we've gotta clear this thing!"

"Time to show off our teamwork!"

This was a very different fight from the trash mobs, so they braced themselves, weapons at the ready.

No sooner had they done so than the Machine God's lasers turned on them and fired a massive beam. Even with Martyr's Devotion, Sally figured it would be a good idea to avoid soaking a direct hit. She leaped away, landing in front of the one passage without a laser cannon—the one leading to the exit circle.

Maple was at the center of the room, bathed in so many laser beams that it was impossible to see her.

"You still there?"

"Yep! The weapons broke off, but I'm not taking damage! Whoa?"

But as she spoke, Maple went flying back toward Sally's position. On pure reflex, Sally caught her—but was unable to stop the momentum. They both went flying.

"Crap, we're gonna land on the exit circle!"

"Eep?! Uh, H-Heaven's Throne!"

Maple threw out her throne in lieu of brakes. A very versatile skill.

It acted as an immobile wall, and they crashed headlong into it. But at least that stopped the boss's knockback from forcibly ejecting them from the fight itself.

"Okay, now what?"

"Last time, it also liked slamming me against walls."

The exit circle was behind them, the passage to the fore, and the open chamber beyond. The Machine God was aiming its weapons directly ahead, firing projectiles with powerful knockback, so they were left pressed up against the throne. Even if they managed to reenter the chamber, they'd be in line of sight for the laser cannons.

"Uh, there's gonna be more bosses after this…so it's best we save what we can."

"Seems like we've got time to think, so let's sit here and plan!"

"Our classic mid-fight strategy session."

Used to it by now, Sally started assessing their options. Maple's defense bought them all the time in the world. Stopping to take stock of the situation allowed them to get on the same page before taking further action—perhaps one of Maple's greatest hidden strengths.

"Looks like Martyr's Devotion reaches just outside the end of the passage, so you can try stuff."

"Mm-hmm. From what I saw, the lasers don't have knockback,

so if I can avoid the Machine God's projectiles, I can get out of here."

"Right."

"I'll dodge those and run down the hall. If that goes well, I'll used Substitute once I've got something other than hallway behind me."

"Got it!"

With Martyr's Devotion, a failed attempt wouldn't be fatal; worst-case scenario, they'd just get knocked back to the throne.

"Okay, here goes. Ice Pillar!"

Sally dropped some ice in front of her, blocking the bombardment and sidestepping the knockback effect.

But placing a blockade in a passage this narrow just focused the projectiles on either side and didn't really let her get anywhere. Sally slapped her cheeks once and took a big breath. That alone told Maple what she was about to do—so she offered encouragement.

"You show him!"

"Will do!"

Sally canceled the Ice Pillar, and high-velocity rounds sped their way.

"Hah...!"

With a quick exhalation, Sally twisted out of their path. It might not look like there were any gaps to wriggle through, but there was a brief time lag between each shot, and she slipped through the openings that made. It looked more like the shots were curving around *her*.

Those she couldn't dodge, she batted attacks aside with her daggers. Moving ceaselessly forward as if the hundreds of rounds were not even there.

"I think Maple's better with these guns than the boss is."

At the end of the passage, she slid sideways under the bombardment, escaped the passage, and used Substitute to swap positions with Maple.

"Wow! Amazing! First try!"

"I just gotta make another run to get back to you! If you can draw most of the fire, I'd appreciate it!"

"Gotcha! Taunt!"

All the laser and gunfire was focused on Maple, bouncing off her. She knew nothing here could hurt her and remained unfazed. No longer threatened by the barrage, Sally calmly walked back down the corridor to freedom.

"Whew, escape complete. Time to fight back!"

"Sally, what now?"

She could barely hear Maple's voice over the sound of bullets hitting her.

"Lasers first! They don't hurt, but they're distracting!"

"Yeah, I can't even see!"

"If they start shooting me, you aim for them, too!"

"Sure!"

If the incoming fire was a bit less relentless, Maple could redeploy her own artillery. At the same time, her weapons weren't nearly as durable as she was. They shattered the second she deployed them, which wasn't exactly helpful.

Sally dropped an Ice Pillar in front of Maple, figuring if anything went wrong, that would at least give her enough cover to allow a partial deployment. Then she started taking out the laser cannons one at a time.

"Quintuple Slash!"

Just as her Double Slash landed sixteen hits, Quintuple Slash now did forty. Each hit might not do much damage, but the strength came from the sheer number of hits delivered in a fraction of the time it would ordinarily take.

The result was absurd burst damage—enough to vaporize the cannon.

"Surprisingly fragile! Next!"

She moved on, and as she shattered the second weapon, the guns turned on Sally—since she was actively destroying things, she must have drawn aggro away from Maple.

"Cool!" Sally grinned. "Shattering them one by one is a real hassle, so this works just fine."

She leaped above the focused laser fire, made a platform in midair, and deflected all incoming rounds with her daggers.

Sparks flew, the clang of metal on metal echoing, but not one damage effect was to be seen. Sally kept dodging lasers, drawing attacks—and free to act again, Maple got her weapons ready.

"Full Deploy! Commence Attack!"

Maple's bristling artillery began blasting the laser cannons.

Just as the Machine God had summoned all these laser cannons, Maple's skill of the same name let her do something very similar.

Maple in full offensive mode was awesome—even if Sally wasn't on the defensive, they could still take out their enemies.

Maple's blanket fire made every laser cannon explode at once, leaving only the main Machine God standing.

"Maple! Hit it hard before anything happens!"

"Got it!"

Maple turned her guns toward it, and Sally dashed in close, throwing out a combo.

"Sextuple Slash!"

A core combo skill she'd been using since day one. Simplistic motion, no added effects, but that was all she needed.

Fire and ice danced with her blows, accelerating her damage.

But as she racked up dozens of hits, that gave the boss time to turn its guns on her.

"Cover Move! Heavy Body!"

Maple saw that coming and warped to Sally's side, ensuring Martyr's Devotion soaked the damage. She was still getting used to Heavy Body, but using that skill allowed her to negate the knockback. The downside was that she could no longer move at all, but since Sally had them right up against the boss, there was nothing stopping Maple from joining the offensive.

"Lure of the Deep!"

She turned one arm into tentacles, crushing the Machine God's torso and doing even more damage than Sally's combo. With her guns practically touching its body, she ripped holes through the Machine God. Its HP dropping like a stone, the boss deployed even more weapons against them.

"But you're going down first! Leap! Pinpoint Attack!"

Sally vaulted directly above the Machine God, spun in the air, and swung her daggers down. They split the body from the head down to halfway through the torso, and the glowing gun barrels collapsed with the boss itself.

"Nice!"

"Yeah, you too, Maple. Five more Devours left. How you doing on weapons?"

"Plenty more to go!"

"Then once Heavy Body runs out, we should move to the center of the room."

"Got it! Let's hope the next wave waits until then."

"I have a hunch I know what's coming, but this should be fun to fight with you."

"Let's knock 'em dead!"

"You know we will. Nothing can handle us."

*　　*　　*

They got ready for the next fight and waited. If nothing else came, great. But they'd called it—the next monster appeared dead ahead.

"Urgh…!"

"I hate to say I told you so."

This was a boss from the fourth stratum—the ogre ruler. The one Maple had received her Pandemonium skill from. Or at least a boss who looked just like him—this time, he was wielding a massive katana every bit as big as he was.

"Is this just a top-difficulty boss rush, or is it specifically picking monsters you soloed?"

"It's not using the same weapon!"

"Then be extra careful."

Sally raised her daggers, and Maple turned her tentacles back into an arm, bracing her shield. The ogre raised its katana.

An instant later, it closed the gap with superhuman speed, unleashing a horizontal slash designed to cleave them both in two.

"……!"

"Unh…yikes?!"

Sally's honed evasion skills meant she managed to duck under the swing.

Maple had her shield in her left hand, so by pure coincidence, she managed to guard. Devour activated but failed to break the blade. She took no damage, either, but its inhuman strength lifted her off the ground, and she went flying toward the wall.

Meanwhile, Sally's instincts were screaming that this boss was one of the toughest foes the game had to offer. She used her crouching position to rocket forward, daggers swinging. With the Machine God, she'd used skills, prioritizing DPS, but here she stuck to regular attacks so she'd have freedom to move. The ogre's reflexes were no joke, and it blocked her attack.

"You beat *this*? Good god. But this time I'm fighting with you!" And what could be more fun? A strong foe and Maple by her side. That gave Sally an unexpected thrill, and she could feel her focus intensify with the feeling.

Their blades clashed against each other. It was blocking every one of Sally's attacks, but she returned that favor. Yet if this continued… Sally was only human. It was only a matter of time before her hyperfocus would falter, and she'd make a mistake.

She needed an opening—which came in the form of a laser beam, fired from the dust cloud obscuring Maple's impact zone.

"Sally!"

The ogre reacted in time, holding up its blade to block the laser—but Sally knew why Maple had called her name, and instantly stepped in, twisting her body to slash the ogre's torso in passing. Maple had given her a shot, and she wasn't about to waste it.

Despite the damage, the ogre took a step toward Maple. Sally saw its legs tensing and quickly darted ahead of it.

"Superspeed!"

The instant before it launched itself forward, Sally got in its way, blocking with both daggers a swing the eye could barely see.

"Where're you going? You're fighting me."

Maple couldn't keep up with *this* speed. That meant Sally would have to be the one deflecting its swings. Since Martyr's Devotion was in place, there was little risk of unfortunate slipups—now she just needed to avoid piercing damage.

"Maple, if you make an opening, I can down it!"

"Gotcha!"

This time, Maple was not alone. With a partner like Sally, she had far more options.

"Commence Assault!"

The moment it reacted to Maple, Sally closed in to hit it. If she was even a moment too late recovering, she'd be unable to handle the boss's response—but when she was this focused, that was a mistake she'd never make.

"It's damn strong, but with us together, it doesn't stand a chance."

The fourth-stratum version was solo-only, but division of labor made a huge difference. This ogre moved far faster than any ordinary player, but so did Sally. Maple kept firing, and Sally didn't once let the ogre go after her friend, keeping it pinned to the spot. That feat alone was beyond the ken of mortal man.

Simple but incredibly difficult teamwork that steadily wore away at the ogre's HP. It took a step back, and purple flames coated the area. And as they did, a big dog emerged from the passage farther back, alight with that same purple fire. It moved to the ogre's side.

Sally backed off, joining Maple.

"Did this happen last time?" she asked.

"Nope! It used the fire, but this feels different. I could handle the fire, but its weapon was doing piercing damage."

Maple had been knocked aside at the start, and they hadn't had a second to chat until the boss finally eased off on its assault.

"I'm mostly gonna keep on it. Counting on Martyr's Devotion to handle the fire. It's likely an AOE."

"Right."

"Sword Dance is at max stack, so I'm doing solid damage."

"And my defense can handle anything that goes wrong!"

Both nodded once, then faced the ogre again.

It now had that fiery dog with it—a big difference from Maple's previous fight. It was two-on-two, so their numbers advantage had vanished. They'd have to be careful.

Both sides watched closely, waiting for the other to act. The boss moved first—the fire dog charged.

"Commence Assault!"

It was charging straight at her, so Maple unloaded in its face. But since it was made of fire, her bullets passed right through, doing no damage.

"Flash Spout!"

Sally made a torrent of water shoot out of the ground, but it dodged with animal-like reflexes. It howled, and the ground around them glowed red.

"We're good! Unbreakable Shield!"

No sooner had the words left Maple's mouth than a pillar of fire enveloped them. Maple knew from experience that fire was less likely to be piercing than apply a damage-over-time effect. Just in case, she'd used a skill that reduced damage taken, but they survived this attack entirely unscathed. It wasn't the kind of attack that could activate Devour, so they didn't really need to worry about *this*.

"Whew!"

"Mm, we can largely just ignore it."

Talking inside the pillar of fire, they took a step forward. As they did, a katana thrust into the wall of fire, blocking their vision. On pure reflex, Sally slapped her daggers against the side of the blade, just barely pushing it off course—and it still gouged Maple's shoulder, prompting a spray of damage sparks.

Even with Unbreakable Shield's powerful damage reduction still in effect, this took out nearly 60 percent of Maple's HP. Sally instantly decided to evac.

"Rapids!"

She grabbed Maple and broke through the wall of fire, riding the rushing water and trying to gain distance. But both ogre and dog were hot on their heels.

"Maple, let's dive!"

"Ground Cradle!"

To give them time to recover, Maple used a skill that pulled them both into the earth.

"Whew... Heal."

"Thanks. Ugh, I knew he'd be strong."

"Yeah, if I've gotta dodge the fires, that'll get rough, so I definitely need Martyr's Devotion handling that."

"Right, right."

"In return, I'll make sure to guard against any further piercing attacks. I'll be *your* shield, Maple."

In other words, each was responsible for negating attacks the other couldn't handle. With Sally going all out on defense, Maple would have to pick up the slack on offense.

"But it blocks my bullets with that sword."

"Don't worry, just hit it when it's open. And if you've gotten up close and personal, how's it gonna block?"

If firing from range let it get its sword up, then she'd just have to stick the barrels to its chest. Like Sally's own attacks, it was physically impossible to avoid everything.

"You relax and keep firing. I won't let it get to you."

"Okay! You'll keep me covered?"

"You know it."

They could both be a sword or a shield. With a plan of attack drawn up, the skill ran out, and they surfaced. The ogre had been waiting for this and was already swinging its blade.

Sally blocked that, precisely deflecting a flurry of slashes, vertical and horizontal.

"You're not getting past me again!"

"It's payback time!"

Sally and the ogre were grinding guards, and Maple turned an arm into a cannon, putting it flat against the ogre's belly, firing. A clean hit and a flurry of damage sparks. A world of pain. The ogre jumped away and, in lieu of counterattacking, had the dog howl, once more trapping them in a pillar of fire.

"I've seen this trick already."

It didn't matter that she couldn't see the attack coming. Sally was utterly confident, daggers at the ready—and once more, the katana thrust into the inferno.

Sally swung both blades, slamming the katana downward and off course.

And the next thing she saw was the ogre bearing down on her—a second katana in its other hand.

"Nice try...!"

Unbalanced from the hard hit, Sally forced herself to recover, crossing her blades and catching the slash on them. But one sword against two daggers was hardly a fair contest.

"Saturating Chaos!"

If one was in trouble, the other stepped up. Maple intentionally attacked from range to bait the ogre into blocking it, giving Sally a moment to right herself—which she turned into a slash against the ogre's side, slipping around behind it.

Since this *was* a boss rush, this ogre didn't have all *that* much HP. A few more solid hits, and they'd be done.

"Maple!"

As she slipped past the boss, Sally glanced back, making eye contact.

Maple knew just what Sally wanted, and she took action.

"Cover Move!"

This warped her to Sally's side. Unlike Substitute, this wasn't technically a teleport; it just made her close the gap incredibly fast.

Which let her take *some* action on the way.

"Ha!"

As she passed the ogre's flank while speeding toward Sally, Maple slammed her shield right up against its side. Naturally, that activated Devour. An eruption of damage sparks flew. An ordinary monster would have been one-shot, and even a boss would not get off lightly—yet the ogre still stood. With Maple off-balance from her attack, the boss raised both blades, swinging her way.

"Your power against my speed!"

As it turned to strike Maple, the ogre was briefly unable to do anything *else*. And Sally dove past, slashing its flank again.

"Substitute!"

Maple and Sally instantly swapped places. Maple was now facing a defenseless back, and Sally found two blades swinging her way.

"Once more!"

This time Maple's shield swallowed up the torso—and as it did, Sally felt the crushing weight of the swords fade away.

"Looks like our teamwork wins," she said, watching the flames die down, as pleased as she was satisfied.

◆□◆□◆□◆□◆

"Whew, we won!"

"Yeah, it worked out."

"Definitely better with two! It was way harder on the fourth stratum."

That time, she'd used up all her skills and been forced to resort to Break Core.

But this time, she still had Indomitable Guardian, Atrocity, and Devour left. Naturally, this was a different place, and not quite the same boss, but this feat was clearly accomplished thanks to the company she'd kept.

"Well, I'm happy to hear it. I know we say this all the time, but Martyr's Devotion really is a game changer."

"Eh-heh-heh, you're welcome."

"There can't be many enemies *that* strong…"

"So what's next?"

They waited a bit, and then a six-winged angel entered through the main passage, with smaller two-winged angel archers appearing from the others.

"You know 'em, Maple?"

"They look a bit like the one I got the throne from, but…not quite."

As they spoke, the angels took the initiative, drawing their bows. Meanwhile, the air around the boss lit up, generating a swarm of arrows made of light that descended upon them. Quite a deadly opening move, but Sally slipped right through the storm, one eye on Maple.

"Oh… You okay, Maple?"

"I'm hunky-dory!"

If these weren't piercing, then no matter how many arrows there were, Maple didn't care.

"Cool. Then guess we go one at a time."

"Yup! But they *can* shatter my weapons, so… Sally, you're up."

"Mm-hmm. Ice Pillar!"

Sally threw out her skill near one of the smaller angels, then used webs to yank herself over, kicking off the pillar and slashing at the angel from the air above. She'd put a twist into it, and her daggers hit hard, scoring a clean hit, and doing so much damage that it was a one-hit kill.

"Cool, flimsier than I thought."

Figuring she'd keep it going, she created a new Ice Pillar and put down a second angel.

Since they'd been fighting all out since they got here, Sword Dance had her DPS maxed out. Ordinarily, it was pretty difficult to get that buff stacked this high, but once there, the boost was considerable. If this had been their first battle, perhaps the angels could have survived her blow—but no longer.

Sally was working her way down the row, but then she noticed the first angel reviving itself. Clearly, there was no use taking these things out. Since they weren't doing much—just slightly buffed archery—she'd figured it was worth downing them before they pulled anything worse, but that had clearly been a waste of time.

"Maple, you're handling the arrows from the smaller angels, right?"

"Yeah! There's no weird debuffs or anything!"

It might not be fazing them, but this rain of arrows would be more than enough to threaten any normal player. These angels only looked like mooks because of Maple's innate defense and her protective skill.

"Then let's forget 'em. If we take the boss out, they're probably done for."

Sally came back to solid ground, sticking within range of Martyr's Devotion. She and Maple headed over toward the biggest angel. As they drew near, they were enveloped in a column of light, like judgment from heaven, but it didn't really do anything.

"We seem to have this fight covered."

"Then let's take it out!"

Maple and Sally both had pretty risky fighting styles, and the ease of a fight could vary a lot depending on their compatibility with the opponent in question. But anyone who wanted to pose a threat to them had to start by equipping a piercing attack.

"Quintuple Slash!"

Figuring it was safe to bust out her skills, Sally used a combo.

Fire and water danced around it, and the boss's HP steadily dropped.

But suddenly the air filled with the gentle sound of harps, and the boss's HP began to rise back up.

"Yikes?!"

"Oh, Sally! The other angels have instruments!"

"So that's why. What now?"

Didn't seem like the brute-force approach—trying to do more damage than the angels could heal—was out of the question, but the sheer amount of healing suggested that wasn't the intended strategy.

"If the light arrows weren't shattering your weapons, I'd just have you gun 'em down."

Looking up, that arrow rain was still falling. Didn't seem like there was any chance of it running out of ammo.

"Um..."

"Oh, Sally, I've got an idea!"

"Lay it on me."

Sally listened, liked what she heard, and nodded. With her approval, Maple started setting up.

"Syrup, Awaken! Giganticize! Psychokinesis!"

Once she had her giant turtle floating, she placed it directly overhead. The arrows were now bouncing off its shell and couldn't shatter her weapons. Martyr's Devotion was shouldering all damage Syrup drew, but that only hit Maple herself—not her artillery. They were covering each other.

"I'll blast away at them. Good luck with yours, Sally!"

"I'm on it!"

"Okay. Commence Assault!"

"Sextuple Slash!"

Just as Maple was weak to piercing damage, healing-dependent endurance strategies fell apart when that healing was denied. With its attacks nulled and its healers downed, this boss had no strengths left.

Ordinarily, the healing and AOE arrow attacks would make this a tough boss even for large parties, but in this case, it had met its match.

"Quadruple Slash! Triple Slash!"

Sally was throwing out skill after skill, trying to do as much damage as she could.

Maple alone might struggle to take out the healers and hurt the boss, but with a solid DPS around, this was all over. Great shielders were usually a class dependent on attackers for damage. The fact that this party's tank was also shooting down angels with her ranged attacks was plenty extraordinary.

With all the angels' skills denied, their only recourse was death.

And as the boss shattered into shards of light, Sally murmured, "You gotta bring pierce damage to a Maple fight."

"Heh-heh-heh! Another damage-free victory!"

Without a proper piercing skill, you might as well stay home. The angel's assault had been nothing but an exercise in futility.

With the angels fallen, they waited for the next round.

They'd made good progress through this rush and had plenty of resources left. The bulk of the skills used on the big bosses had been Sally's combo moves, so most of Maple's big guns still had uses left.

"We've got fight left in us!"

"Yeah. Given the pattern, next up is the sixth…"

At this point, the blood drained from Sally's face. The rules here were all too clear, and she had a hunch what they'd be fighting next.

And her fears proved grounded. From the main passage emerged a skeleton wearing a rusty crown, in tattered finery, and leading an undead horde.

"Uh...ummmmm!"

"Retreat! My throne's still out."

Sally had gone from badass to newborn deer in seconds, and Maple pulled her back down the exit circle corridor.

"I-Ice Pillar!"

Temporarily sealing the passage with a wall of ice, Sally clung to Maple, who was perched on her throne.

"This hall's too narrow for Syrup to go giant...and I can't use Predators. They're undead, so poison probably won't do much..."

Maple concluded that Machine God's barrage was pretty much the only way to take advantage of this corridor camp.

ght be temporarily plugging the flow, but soon

ad would come pouring in.

Garden, Sinking Ground."

kely wouldn't instantly kill these things. In which

to slow their progress. Syrup's skills made her

damage and altered the texture of the ground to

's advance.

"Sally, just throw random spells at them! They're all coming from the same direction, so you'll probably hit something!"

"Mm..."

Sally wrapped her scarf around her face, leaning against Maple. Eyes closed but facing the open chamber.

A moment later, the Ice Pillars vanished, and the undead lurched forward, groaning. The boss hung back, buffing its minions, so they'd have to clear out this wall of corpses first.

"Commence Assault!"

Maple's guns spit fire, and the undead started toppling. But it

was hardly one hit each, and they were crawling over literal dead bodies, drawing closer despite the quagmire underfoot.

"Cyclone Cutter! Fire Ball!"

Sally was flinging spells, but she'd only learned the bare minimum magic. It was better than nothing, at least.

"Hng, they're gaining ground."

"Th-they are?!"

"Syrup, Mother Nature!"

The turtle's skill made massive vines grow, the sheer bulk of them knocking the undead away. Possibly to make up for the quantity, these undead didn't have obnoxious conditions like "only vulnerable to magic," and they *were* steadily thinning the numbers.

"Rapids! F-F-Flash Spout!"

Sally produced a flood, and between that and the vines, the undead were swept away. If she allowed them to get close enough to grab her, she might not take damage, but her mind would likely collapse.

"Hmm, not quite enough damage."

Maple thought for a minute, then realized there was still a way Sally could fight.

"Oh, I've got it! I know a way to get you back in the fight!"

"Huh? Wh-wh-what is it?"

Sally didn't see any way she could get in on *this*, but Maple whispered the plan. A reversal of their usual roles, but since Sally was hardly thinking straight, ideas weren't exactly coming her way.

"G-got it. Oboro, Shadow Clone!"

Activating the skill made copies of Sally. She didn't use them all that often because they weren't under her conscious control and could get nailed with piercing damage, turning Martyr's Devotion into an Achilles' heel. But in this case, the lack of direct control was a blessing.

Four identical clones dashed right at the undead, attacking.

"Wow! Sally, fighting ghouls!"

Regardless of what their source was doing, the clones' behavior was set in stone. Ordinarily, their low endurance meant they didn't last long or they ran too far off to keep safe, but with the wall of undead in front of them, they were forced to stay in range of Martyr's Devotion. As long as they stuck by Maple, they were invincible warriors.

"Get 'em!"

The four Sallys were steadily downing undead. This trash mob was not really a threat to her as long as she was psychologically capable of fighting them.

"If the total number is fixed, we can clean them up...but is it?"

Maple decided to conserve ammo, letting the clones go to town. Sally herself was cycling through Ice Pillar, Flash Spout, and Rapids as the cooldowns allowed, focused on keeping the horde at bay.

Sally's Water Wielding skill set was pretty good at pushing opponents away from her. Used right, it also helped her move quickly around the map. The area these skills affected was broad enough to be effective even with her eyes closed.

"H-how's it going, Maple?"

"Pretty great! Keep it up!"

As Maple cheered them on, the clones slowly carved their way through the horde. At last, Maple could see the room beyond again.

The clones all made a beeline for the boss, but that was no longer in range of Martyr's Devotion, so the boss's black flames soon took them out.

"Augh! I can only keep them safe if they're close by! Still, thanks! A real Sally Spectacular."

"Can't claim much credit... Only the boss left?"

"Yep! So far, doesn't seem like he's summoning more."

Since Heaven's Throne covered the entire boss chamber, this type of boss couldn't really use any of its major moves. It wound up slowly creeping toward them, trying to get in range to attack.

"It's getting closer...if it comes down this hall, then I can fight it!"

Maple didn't want to risk getting off her throne. If she stood up and it used a summon skill, they'd be back to square one.

She decided her best bet was to stop shooting and wait for it to come to her.

It had let the clones get pretty close before fighting back, so she felt pretty sure it would at least enter the corridor.

Maple's guess proved right, and, bones clattering, the boss moved down the hall. It was only a few steps away now—close enough to be slowed by Sinking Ground.

"Is it here? Is it here?!"

"Yeah, not far away."

"Then let's kill it! Kill it! Ice Pillar!"

Sally threw out a wall of ice behind it, cutting off the boss's retreat. Now Maple was free to aim her weapons.

"Now nothing can stop me from shooting it!"

"Get it before it gets *here*!"

"That's the plan! Commence Assault!"

Maple's bullets tore through the boss, and Sally's wild spell-flinging went every which way. Soon enough, the boss's HP ran out, and the corpse was no more.

"Skill: Apex of Authority acquired."

The announcement came with the boss's demise. They waited a bit, but no further enemies appeared.

"I think it's over."

"I-it is?! No chance to redeem myself?!"

The whole goal had been teamwork, but the last round hadn't really gone to plan.

Sally removed the scarf from her face but seemed speechless. She kept looking from Maple to where the boss had been.

"But you did a lot! Even in that last fight."

"I just wanted to end it in style."

"We were really looking out for each other."

They'd come here to try out co-op techniques, and arguably, they'd succeeded. Sally had covered Maple's weakness, and Maple had certainly returned that favor.

"Well, I guess. So? Am I still cut out to be your partner?" Sally asked.

Maple just grinned and shot her a thumbs-up.

"You betcha! You were so good against that ogre, I should be asking *you*."

"Heh-heh...Maple, if you didn't qualify, nobody else would."

"Oh? I'm not convinced."

"Yeah. I mean, you're just that strong."

"Eh-heh-heh. Oh! Wasn't there a new skill?"

"We both got that, huh? Lessee..."

Apex of Authority

Summoned monsters now have x1.5 to all stats.

Simple but extremely strong.

"Very seventh stratum. Passive, no downsides, well worth it."

"Yes! Syrup, you got stronger!"

"And from the description, it's not just our tamed monsters. I bet it works on your Predators, too. They've got stats of their own, right?"

"Oh! Everyone's growing!"

"I've got some uses for it, but…I doubt it affects Oboro's Shadow Clone."

"'Cause that isn't *your* skill?"

"Exactly. But I'll have to give it some thought, see how I can work it in. Whew…that last round wore me out. Should we call it a day?"

"Yep!"

Satisfied with their great new skill, they left the dungeon behind.

CHAPTER 4

Defense Build and Hellish Training

After clearing the dungeon with Maple, Sally was sprawled out on the couch at the guild home, eyes closed, deep in thought.

"What's wrong? Not often you look that stressed out."

"Kanade? Oh yeah…just…"

"Thinking about the next PvP event again? Everyone's getting new skills."

Like Sally and Maple, Mai and Yui had found a new strength. They were once again out waving eight hammers each, getting themselves used to their new fighting style, and working on the ninth-event goals.

"What about you, Kanade?"

"I'm building up my stock of grimoires and keeping an eye on the other guilds. Like you said, Thunder Storm have kept their pets top secret."

Kanade's combat potential revolved heavily around grimoires that could be used only once. The rest of his skills weren't particularly noteworthy, so he wasn't really built for the constant fighting required to grind levels. For that reason, he was spending a large chunk of his time observing other players.

"Right. If we knew that, we could form a plan, but..."

"They're interesting. Since their fights are flashy, it's pretty easy to track them down."

Wherever Velvet and Hinata went, lightning fell, cold air gathered, and objects began to float. They were as eye-catching as Maple.

"I figured I'd check out Rapid Fire next."

"Mm-hmm, good luck there."

"I should come back with *something*."

But even as they spoke, part of Sally's mind was clearly on something else. Kanade pondered that for a second.

"Look, if you're stuck on something, best to ask Maple. Later."

With that, he fluttered his fingers and left the guild home.

"Ask Maple, huh?"

Sally pondered it a while longer, then made up her mind and jumped to her feet.

◆□◆□◆□◆□◆

The next day, in the real world after school, Risa got ready to go home, then closed her eyes and took a deep breath. Kaede came running over.

"Risa, what's up?"

"Thinking about swinging by a game shop on the way home."

"Oh? Something new out?"

"No, not like that..."

Risa was being unusually evasive, and Kaede crooked her head.

"Would you...wanna come with?" Risa asked.

"......? Sure, why not?"

This didn't seem like one of Risa's attempts to get her into a new game. Wondering what was going on, Kaede joined her friend, and they headed out.

"Even I know the way by now!"

"Heh…well, it doesn't hurt to see what they've got."

"Ah-ha-ha. I always just end up looking. Hard to tell what's good."

"But that's one way to have fun."

The packages were designed to show off the games, and the backs had *some* descriptive text. Looking those over was enjoyable in its own right. Wandering around the shop, picking up anything that caught the eye—a perfect afternoon.

For that reason, Risa usually picked up speed as she got near the shop, but today she was actually slowing down.

"Are you doing okay?"

"Er, uh…yes."

She sure didn't look it. But when Kaede suggested they turn back, Risa insisted she was fine. That was worrying, but by now, they'd reached the game shop.

"What are you here for?"

"That's the thing…," Risa said, slowly advancing on a particular shelf.

"Huh?!"

Following her gaze, Kaede gasped. The packages and titles lined up there were all horror games.

"S-seriously?"

"Yeah. High time I got over it."

Recent fights had left her cowering; she'd had to skip the entire sixth stratum, and even on other floors, she'd diligently avoided any spooky areas. It was a real detriment, and one she'd rather rid herself of.

"I can't recommend it. You won't be able to sleep!"

"Urgh…"

There was a big gap between a horror area in a regular game and what a dedicated horror game offered. It seemed unlikely that someone shredded by the first could handle the second. Kaede had known Risa a long time, had seen her make these declarations before, and knew they always ended in despair.

"If you insist, I won't stop you, but…"

Given what had *just* happened on the seventh stratum, Maple figured this was doomed to failure. Risa dithered for a long moment, thoughts swirling, but finally made up her mind.

"I-I'm going for it! I've decided!"

"You pick a game yet?" Kaede asked.

Risa took one off the shelf.

"V-VR?! Are you *sure*?"

There was a big difference between that stuff happening on-screen and jumping right into that terrifying experience. Risa had backed herself into a corner, drunk on her own resolve, convinced it would work out—Kaede had seen all this before. But she also knew once Risa got like this, the only way to talk her down was to post results—good or bad.

"This one's two-player…"

"Oh? Ohhh? You're dragging me in?!"

"I—I plan to beat it solo! Just…um, you know."

"Okay, fine! When're we doing this?"

"Between *NewWorld Online* events!"

"Will we need that much time? The package even says it's super scary."

Kaede herself didn't have any particular problems with horror, so she'd taken the box from Risa's hands and was reading the back of it.

"I'm buying it! Deep breath! Okay!"

Calming herself down a bit, Risa headed for the register.

"Good luck!"

"Y-yeah…"

She'd sworn to beat the game solo and didn't wanna go crying for help right away. Clutching the shopping bag tight, she tried to fire herself up.

"Lemme know if you finish!"

"Okay, I'm gonna give it a shot."

Even if she couldn't beat it, she should be able to progress the story a bit. It supported co-op but was mostly a single-player experience.

She'd see Kaede at school the next day and tell her how far she'd gotten.

They walked home, splitting up at the usual corner, and headed to their respective houses. Alone, Risa looked at her bag again, uneasy.

"I can do it...I can! I've gotta get over this!"

She'd set out with the intent of playing as soon as she got back, but where she normally rushed home to start playing, today her feet were like lead.

"I'm home..."

Back in her room, Risa put her things down and changed out of her uniform. She took the horror game from the bag and set it on her desk.

"Okay, then. After dinner."

It was a reasonably lengthy game, so Risa decided to put it off for now and get her homework done first.

"Not that hard once you get the trick," she muttered, whipping through her math problems. They just took a little concentration. Part of her knew why she was so focused, but she pretended she didn't.

She kept finding other things to do, and it started getting dark out. Then she heard that dinner was served, and since her homework was just about done, Risa ran down the stairs to eat.

*   *   *

After dinner, Risa took a bath and went back to her room. Normally, she'd have been playing a game immediately, but when she went to do that—the box's presence couldn't be ignored.

"......Nope, I'm doing it! I said I would..."

But all she actually did was turn it over in her hands.

"Okay, playing it at night's not a great idea. I'll do it right after I get home tomorrow. Yeah."

With that settled, Risa started a different game.

The next day, Risa woke up and went to school like always. Kaede spotted her on the way in and came running over.

"Morning, Kaede."

"Morning, Risa!"

They moved on, chatting. Eventually, Kaede broached the subject.

"Did you play that game at all?"

"Uh, no. Not yet..."

Risa babbled a bit about homework and timing and then looked away.

"......Can we play it together?"

"I figured. Sure! When?"

Assuming the longer they put it off, the less likely she was to ever play the game, Risa suggested this very afternoon.

"Got it. After school today! Do I need anything?"

"Nope, I've got a spare console for two-player."

"Then I'm...looking forward to it? Yeah!"

Risa's goal wasn't exactly to have a good time, so Kaede wasn't sure exactly what to say.

"I've never tried a horror game! You don't exactly own any."

"Ah-ha-ha…and I never suggested any."

Kaede never picked any games out herself, only when Risa suggested them. For that reason, she'd had no occasion to try out horror games.

"Are they scary?"

"Probably? I wouldn't know."

Risa had yet to try one, so she didn't really have tips ready.

"Then we'll just have to find our own fun!"

"If there's fun to be had, yeah."

"Oh…right…"

Firming up plans for after school, they walked the rest of the way in.

When classes ended, Kaede came over to Risa's house.

"I'm home!"

"I'm here, too!"

They went upstairs to Risa's room. Risa had been thinking it through and was once again highly motivated.

"Wait a sec—I'll get us set up."

"Sure thing!"

Maple took a seat, and not long after, Risa had two VR consoles ready.

Kaede picked up one and asked about the game again.

"Um, so creepy crawlies are gonna chase us around?"

"Yep. We get sucked into a pocket dimension and have to solve puzzles to escape."

"Okay, so basically like dungeons."

"Is…it? Well, if we look at it that way, it does feel less intimidating."

The back of the box had several screenshots, and it looked a bit like a hospital.

"I thought I'd choose a setting we don't normally end up in."

Even if she wound up permanently afraid of places like that, it was less of an issue that way. Sort of a negative outlook considering her goal here, but she'd learned from her previous failures.

"Then, shall we? Like we always do, play to the first good stopping point?"

"Yeah...okay..."

Reaching the end of the first chapter had often been their initial goal when trying out new games together. Aiming for that again, they dove into the virtual world.

When they opened their eyes, they found a crumbling desk, chair, and blackboard. The windows were painted over, letting no light in; the room itself was dimly lit by a glow of unknown origin. From what Kaede could see, this felt more like sitting in a classroom.

"Wasn't this supposed to be a hospital?" she asked.

"......? ......??"

But Risa was just looking in every direction, lost.

"Let's start exploring!"

"I—I guess..."

It was very video game-y. Anywhere they could gather items was emphasized, making it hard to overlook even in the darkness. Kaede quickly spotted a highlighted piece of paper on the desk and picked it up.

"Um...mm-hmm, it says, 'The first thing we knew, we were here, and don't know how to leave. It's creepy, but we've got no choice but to look around.' Is there someone else here?"

"Maybe...?"

Risa was clearly rattled by the unexpected setting and already had one foot out the door.

"Guess we'll have a look around ourselves!"

"Okay. Please don't let anything happen…"

It might only be chapter one, but it was chapter one of a horror game, so something was definitely going to happen. Kaede grabbed Risa's hand and pulled her toward the door.

Scoping things out, she opened the door a crack, poked her head through, and looked both ways. Dimly lit corridors in either direction, no sounds, no signs of life. But it was so dark, she couldn't see very far, so she couldn't be sure.

"Seems safe enough?"

"Nothing out there…?"

"I don't think so…but not a hundred percent."

She could normally use Machine God or Hydra to check for enemies and defeat them at the same time, but such violent measures weren't available here.

"Which way?"

"Whichever way seems safer…"

"Uh…then right it is!"

They couldn't exactly stay cooped up in the classroom forever, so Kaede picked a direction and headed down the hall. Since it was a school, they passed more classrooms, but most doors Kaede tried were stuck and wouldn't open.

"Is there a trick to opening them? Wait…"

Kaede peered through the little glass window and saw a girl sitting alone at a desk.

"Oh, look, Risa! There's someone in here!"

Risa timidly opened one eye to see, joining Kaede at the window.

An instant later, the girl's face shot up, turning toward them.

Then she vanished—and hands suddenly slammed against the window, accompanied by banging and screaming.

"Yikes!"

"Eeee…!"

Jet-black eyes against pale, lifeless skin stared back at them. Kaede concluded that they should leave. She tried to help Risa back to her feet.

"W-we should run!"

"……"

Risa seemed out of it, so Kaede pulled her back the way they'd come. She glanced over her shoulder, but there was nothing spooky on their heels.

"Whew…we're safe! That was a shocker!"

She'd certainly been surprised, but they'd gotten away clean, so Kaede just looked relieved.

"In this game, I'm plenty fast! Running away isn't hard at all!"

She tried to put a positive spin on things. Kaede was braced for the next encounter, but Risa was already on the verge of tears.

"Uh, what do you wanna do?" Kaede asked.

"I-I'm fine! Keep going!"

Risa forced the words out, hell-bent on getting through this. She managed to get her legs back under her and took a few deep breaths.

"I s-swore I'd get over this hang-up!"

But having Kaede with her was the only reason she'd managed to pick herself up. On her own, not only was that impossible, she'd never even have managed to boot the game up.

"Okay! Then let's try left!"

"Y-yeah…whew…okay."

Kaede pulled her the other way down the hall, checking each room. They found several more tutorial notes giving them guidance. These explained how to use the items they'd find here to help them escape. One item in particular seemed vital.

"Oh! Risa, look! Flashlights!"

Kaede flicked hers on and off, and Risa made sure hers worked, too.

"Much easier to explore now!"

"Yeah...even a bit of light is better than darkness."

They directed the flashlight beams around the room—then heard something approaching outside. They quickly shut off the flashlights. An EKG graph appeared at the top right of their view, like a status effect; as the thing outside drew closer, the waves on it grew larger.

"""............"""

They crouched quietly behind the podium, and the waves gradually died down. Eventually, the graph vanished.

"Whew, it didn't catch us! Guess we've gotta be careful with the lights."

According to a diary they'd found, this ghost was patrolling the school, and they had to avoid it while searching for clues to escape. This might be a pretty realistic game, but it was still a game—there were systems built in to help players avoid the ghost.

Using lights meant it could find them easier, but some items could be found only when the lights were on.

"Let's scope this floor out!"

"Mm..."

"Ah-ha-ha, we've totally swapped roles."

Risa knew so much about games that she was usually the one offering suggestions, but that didn't apply to horror. And Kaede had spent enough time around Risa that some of those leadership skills had rubbed off on her.

"Yeah...I'm hanging on by a thread here," Risa admitted.

"Oh? Well, I've got your back!"

"Good. Thank you."

Checking the EKG to ensure the ghost wasn't nearby, they crept out of the classroom. They went room to room, searching for a way out, but the school was three stories tall. The items and maps they found worked just like the inventory in *NewWorld Online*, so at least they didn't have to worry about dropping anything.

"Risa, over here!"

A while into their search, Kaede saw the meter pop up and hastily shut off her flashlight. She and Risa hid themselves.

"Did it spot us?"

"Please don't spot us; please don't spot us…"

Risa shut her eyes, waiting for the hand fate dealt them. Kaede was doing her best to monitor the situation. After a while, the ghost started moving away, and she let out a sigh of relief.

"Whew…that was stressful! Are all horror games like this?"

"……Urgh."

This was definitely not the kind of stress Risa handled well. She looked wiped.

"Wanna call it a day after the next classroom? We've been playing awhile, and this school seems like it'll take forever to get through."

They'd explored most of the second floor but had yet to venture through the other two. Their goal had been the end of chapter one, but Risa's soul looked ready to leave her body.

"Mm-hmm, sounds good. Let's do that."

"All righty then! Only place left on this floor is the art room!"

When they were sure the ghost wouldn't find them, they slipped down the hall, making it safely to the art room. They swept the interior with their flashlights.

"Wow, so many canvases!"

"Anything here?"

"Statues, paintings, palettes... Um, oh!"

"Wh-what?"

Risa's eyes kept snapping shut anytime anything happened, so Kaede pulled her over to the item indicator. She found some keys with a tag attached.

"Oh, that's an obvious clue! Um...the science lab?"

Picking up the key automatically collected it, storing it in her inventory. This was the only key to be seen, but at least they had their next destination.

"There was no science lab on this floor, so this seems like a good place to stop."

"Then let's save and quit!"

There were several save points around the map, and they'd just saved before coming to the art room. They just had to make it back there, and they could stop for the day.

"Then follow me! Careful not to trip!"

Risa was no longer opening her eyes at all, but Kaede held out a hand, and she took it. Risa sighed, certain she'd made it through.

Kaede took a step forward, and Risa a step after her—and something cold wrapped around her free hand.

"Huh...?"

Startled, Risa turned around—and found a girl in a school uniform. The cold grasp was this girl's translucent hand.

"Don't go... *Don't gooo!*"

Inky black trails dripping from her eyes, the ghost pulled Risa's arm with both hands. The shock of this overwhelmed Risa's capacity for fear, and she couldn't even shake the ghost off. She crumpled to the ground.

"Urp? Wh-wh-wh-what? Risa?!"

Kaede had spun around, not recognizing this ghost's voice, but when she tried to help Risa, all she could see was black—and then the words Game Over appeared.

When her vision cleared, their inventory was back to before they'd hit the art room. It had automatically loaded their last save.

Risa was sitting silently on the floor, unable to stand. She did not seem capable of going to the art room again.

"Let's stop here!" Kaede said and pulled up the menu. She hit the EXIT button and sent them both back to the real world.

Outside the game, she removed her VR headset and considered her first horror-game experience. Since it was VR, it had felt much like a haunted house; she'd certainly been startled a few times but had largely enjoyed the tension of sneaking around.

"Risa?" she said, helping her friend remove the headset.

"Kaede…," Risa said, looking exhausted.

"What?"

"I'm *never* getting over this."

Tears welled up in her eyes, and she sounded defeated. Kaede had seen this coming, so she just nodded.

"See? I told you so! This happens every time you try and get over it."

"You can have this game…if you want it…"

"Hmm…I don't think so. I'm not really up for playing multiple things at once like you do, and it seemed sorta long."

"Okay…sorry I dragged you into this."

"Not a problem. It was all new to me! Kinda neat. But I'd better start heading home."

Between watching out for the ghosts, Kaede being new to leading the way, and Risa's reluctance to move around, quite a bit of time had passed, and it was getting dark out. Kaede picked up her backpack and made sure she wasn't forgetting anything.

"Mm, good night."

"Yep! Hey, what time you gonna call me?"

"Huh? Oh…"

Kaede already knew Risa wasn't going to sleep much, so she anticipated the call. This same thing had happened on the sixth stratum, and given how this horror game had turned out, the call was inevitable.

Catching her drift, Risa squirmed uncomfortably but couldn't insist it wouldn't happen.

"M-maybe around ten?" she managed.

"Cool."

Kaede said her goodbyes and headed home. Left behind, Risa collapsed on her desk, both hands mussing her hair.

"What a disaster! I'm such an idiot!"

How many times was she going to make this same mistake? Worse, why was she always so certain this time she could pull it off?

"Never again! This is the last time!"

Risa shot the horror game's box a baleful glare.

CHAPTER 5

Defense Build and the Trickster

A few days after the ill-fated horror-game attempt, the long ninth event was nearing the halfway mark. The total event monster kill count was already nearing the ultimate goal.

"Way faster than I thought."

"Yeah, and materials aren't that hard to get. I've almost got enough."

"Looks like we'll get there without me really contributing much," Kanade said.

He was with Chrome and Iz, looking over the standings. At this point, they'd clearly reach the goal even if they just left things to the most active guilds and killed only what they stumbled across anyway.

"I guess I'll just keep on checking out the other guilds."

"Oh, spying on them?"

"What I've heard about Rapid Fire's main duo sounds interesting. Thought I'd see them for myself."

"They're pretty tough. The more we know, the better we'll do in PvP."

"Exactly. I'll let you know if anything comes up."

"Yes, if you need anything, don't hesitate to ask."

"Mm. Oh, and it seemed like Sally had a lot on her mind. I thought it was PvP-related, but she didn't specify—follow up on that for me if you see her."

"Will do."

"I'll bear it in mind."

Between his grimoire collection and Sou's Mimic skill, Kanade was a versatile fighter. He wasn't that high-level but was good at using skills to make up the difference. His build was highly dependent on Akashic Records and the grimoires it generated, and he'd struggle to fight much on the seventh layer without them. If there was info out there that would help decide which grimoires to keep, he wanted to know it.

Kanade left the guild home in search of intel on Lily and Wilbert. Not long after, Maple and Sally came in.

"Oh, you just missed each other."

"Yup, a minute later and he could have asked directly."

"......? What's this about?"

"Oh, Kanade just said you were worrying about PvP and hoped we'd pick your brain on it."

"Were you, Sally?"

"I last talked to Kanade... Erp?!"

Sally made a noise, then clapped a hand to her mouth, faking a cough.

"Y-you okay there?"

"Uh, never mind that. I was worrying about something else; sounds like I misled him. My bad!"

"Oh? Ohhh." Maple figured it out and started nodding. Sally shot her a glare, warning her to say nothing, so she kept her lips sealed.

"Then fine. Didn't mean to pry!"

"Yeah, sorry we asked. I'll let Kanade know."

"Good idea. Please."

Chrome and Iz went back to their own conversation.

"Was this about the horror game?" Maple whispered.

"Argh! Why'd you have to be so perceptive *now* of all times?"

Sally hid her expression beneath her scarf.

Meanwhile, as he had promised, Kanade was scoping out the Rapid Fire leaders. Lily and Wilbert always hunted monsters at the same place at the same time, like they were doing target practice. Despite the sheer number of stratums and the size of them, it was relatively easy to track them down.

"I didn't really learn anything worth mentioning about Thunder Storm, so let's hope I get lucky here."

He had Sou out in case of sudden monster attacks and, like Sally, was moving around the field on horseback.

With his mirror slime around, he could have it copy him and fight without depleting his grimoires. Outside of important events and boss fights, he was leaving most combat to his pet.

As he neared the location Maple and Sally had first met Rapid Fire, he got off his horse and sat down with his back against a tree, observing them through binoculars.

"Every bit as accurate as I heard...and very strong hits. I bet I couldn't even get close."

Wilbert was fighting enemies that flew, and not one of his arrows missed. This lent credence to the idea his hits were guaranteed. And each hit was strong enough to slay their targets; any ordinary player would be a pincushion before they got anywhere near him.

"You'd have to pull out all the stops. The right skills, and tons of AGI."

And if you ran at him from the front, he'd back off just as quick. Like Sally said, the way the monsters exploded suggested high attack, but his delicate footwork and nimble evasion proved his stats weren't nearly as extreme as the twins'.

He had range, power, and mobility—just being so balanced made him objectively *good*. It would not be easy to take him down.

"And he's got Lily with him. Yep, no way in."

Rapid Fire's leaders were each a force to be reckoned with, and that only got worse when they were backing each other up.

Wilbert's arrows were instant one-hit kills. When Lily was attacking, she handled greater numbers with superior firepower. With the other providing backup, it would be hard to strike their blind spot. This was a pair that excelled at all aspects of the game. A very different type of strength from what Velvet and Hinata had.

Solving a puzzle Iz had made for him with one hand, Kanade watched to see if they'd summon their pets or use a skill they hadn't shown off yet. Eventually, they stopped shooting and came his way.

"Oh! Today we have a fascinating spectator."

"I do apologize. Lily insisted we come over."

"Well, I'm the one acting like a spy. You do impress. I kept myself pretty far away."

These were Iz-crafted high-power binoculars, and he'd been at the extreme end of their range, so he found it hard to believe they'd spotted him with the naked eye.

"Ha-ha, Will's one-of-a-kind."

"I'm afraid I can't exactly explain the how...but I will confirm I *did* spot you."

That left Kanade scratching his head. Clearly, Sally's instincts

had been right on target. Wilbert had some skill or rare item that gave him eyesight the equal or better than binoculars made by a top-tier crafter.

"Ha-ha, nobody's getting the drop on you."

"Heh-heh, that's the goal. I appreciate you not mincing words."

Lily shot him a confident smile. What he knew about Wilbert's talents was all broad strokes and didn't lend itself to counter-strategizing. In which case, she likely concluded they would come out ahead.

"I'm just doing a little scouting. My guild has you marked as *notable*."

"Oh, stop, you're making me squirm."

"Not me!" Lily said. "I think it's a fair evaluation."

"Is it?"

"Now you're being coy. You could have backed me up."

"Could I?"

"We're off topic." She turned back to Kanade. "Did you learn anything valuable?"

"I've certainly confirmed how vast your enemy-detection range is and your archery skills."

"Ah. But really, that's everything, isn't it? It can't be beat."

"Yes…I'm certainly at a disadvantage."

"If Will merely leaves you at a disadvantage, you're doing all right."

If he just tore through grimoires without a thought to the future, Kanade might manage it, but if Wilbert had more cards up his sleeve, he was done for. That's why he'd called it a disadvantage.

"Naturally, we don't mind being watched. But we've more or less shown your guild master everything we're inclined to share."

"Mm, so I've heard. I said I was scouting, but it's at least half just personal curiosity. It's fun seeing what skills are out there and how players master them."

"Aha."

"That sounds genuine. And I guess I get it."

"So if you plan on fighting more, I'll stick around to watch. It's certainly satisfying seeing monsters shot down that quickly."

"Oh yeah? But I'm afraid we're wrapping up for the day."

"Ha-ha-ha, no worries. I'm the one who came to you. You'd be well within your rights to run me off."

If they were done, then Kanade would just go check out someone from another guild.

But as he got ready to do so, there was a splashing sound, and all three turned toward it. They found water spraying out of the ground, spreading fast—already a solid ten yards across, far too large to call a puddle.

"Hmm, is this your skill?"

"Not mine."

"I have no memory of this skill in my repertoire and I'd say the same goes for the rest of our guild members."

They looked around but saw no other players—and the current event *was* aquatic.

"Will, have any sharks, octopuses, or eels shown any indications of this?"

"Not that I noticed. I've yet to encounter any monsters that had a skill like this."

"Right, then let's give it a minute. Kanade, we'd appreciate you sticking around. After all, no telling what'll happen."

Given the scale of the deepening waters, Lily figured this was a big deal. If there were reinforcements conveniently nearby, it made sense to rope them in.

"Mm, why not? I like it. The surprise just makes it better."

Kanade stuck around, and the three of them watched carefully as the puddle continued to spread. In time, ripples began radiating from the center; then there was a splash, and a giant squid shot out, hovering in the air.

"Gosh. We haven't seen a giant squid since the second event."

"I like it! No clue what it's doing here, but it's a big one. Let's get it, Will!"

"But of course."

"It's not underwater, and I'm stronger now—I've got options."

In the second event, Kanade had been thrown into the water and instagibbed by a giant squid. This wasn't the same monster, but it was a good chance to prove how much he'd grown.

All three raised their weapons. They began by buffing their main offense, Wilbert.

"Able Aide, Tactical Tutelage, Transcendent Power, Venerable Command, Take Heart, Advice."

"Sou, Mimic."

The slime had been resting on Kanade's head, but now it hopped down, shifting shapes to look exactly like Kanade himself. Lily's eyes went wide, immediately curious.

"So *that's* your monster? I've heard stories, but seeing it in person is still astounding."

"It's handy, especially with my build."

Kanade had Sou summon its grimoires and used a bunch that improved damage. The effects were weaker if Sou cast them, but Kanade was constantly collecting good skills without meeting the tough acquisition criteria, so the resulting buffs were still significant.

"I'm the only Maple Tree member who can really buff anyone. Gotta do my bit."

"Ha-ha-ha…these numbers are more than a 'bit.' Thank you. Time I took my shot."

Will raised his bow, drawing the string taut. Aiming right between the squid's eyes.

"Drawn Taunt. Annihilation Arrow."

A dark-red glow...and at speeds the eye could barely follow, the arrow shot through the squid's bulk, vanishing into the sky beyond. A geyser of damage sparks followed, but the HP bar above its head barely budged.

"Whoa... Well, okay."

"Most unexpected. Lily, care to lead?"

"Yeah, I'd better. But it sure doesn't *look* that tough..."

If Wilbert was unable to down a foe on the first shot, his subsequent damage was considerably reduced. In which case, they used Quick Change to swap out their equipment and made Lily their primary attacker.

She immediately summoned an army and went on the offensive, but given how little damage their deadly archer had done, her approach wasn't exactly efficient.

"Counter coming...Guard Heart."

"Sou! Enhance Function, Spirit Light, Guardian Barrier."

Tentacles were swooping in from both sides, trying to crush them all. Kanade threw out some damage-reduction skills, and Lily had all her troops rush to tank the blow. But even with the damage reduced, its power was off the charts. The soldiers stood their ground momentarily before crumbling.

"Worse than I thought! Rapid Factory! Reproduction!"

These were two skills that Sally had not mentioned to Kanade; they resupplied the troops as fast as they were decimated and shored up the walls.

"Oh, you can summon that quickly?"

"That I can. You saw how good Will is. If I wish to stand by his side, this is the bare minimum."

"Ha-ha, I've set no such requirements. Though I certainly appreciate your contributions."

"Still, this means we can't fight back. Will, call in the guild. We need backup."

"Understood. I'll see who's available."

"I'll contact my guild as well."

"Good to hear! Go for it."

Lily promised she could hold out until help arrived—and her flood of troops *was* staving off the tentacles.

Still, they were pretty far from town, and it would take a while for reinforcements to arrive.

"Without Sou's damage reduction, this would be tough. Will and I are both focused on buffing offense, which hurts us here."

"I'm not exactly stocked up myself. I can only soak this a few more times."

"That's plenty. Oh! Will, unexpected help."

Players in the area had spotted the giant squid and come to take a closer look. They were hesitating, not wanting to jump in uninvited, so Lily called out to them.

"This just showed up! Not a boss a small party can handle! Do you mind lending a hand?"

Giant bosses like this didn't usually roam the fields, so no one was sure of the protocol. Now, they all started attacking—and that helped draw aggro away from the three of them, letting them escape the tentacles' grasp.

"Whew, so close to getting crushed. Thank god for your damage reduction."

"Mm, seeing your defenses firsthand is payment enough."

"My build's all about summoning. Of course I manage *that*."

"But seeing is believing. Now I'm *sure* you can weather most threats."

"I won't deny that."

"Looks like our nearest guild members are almost here."

"The more the merrier. Look, those new arrivals just got blown away."

A top player like Lily had been forced to play defensively despite having Kanade and Wilbert backing her, so it stood to reason most people couldn't handle it.

About a third of the incoming players had already fallen victim to the tentacles. It was hovering and hard to approach—definitely a boss some players would struggle with at the best of times.

"But mages can stand back and throw spells. You've both got ranged attacks, so...should we join the offense?"

"I'd rather not have it come after us again. Let's not go too hard until more people arrive."

"Yeah, fair enough."

Lily summoned more soldiers and had them fire at the squid. Kanade had Sou use a few high-level grimoires.

"Sou, Blend."

Kanade explained that this would make them less likely to draw aggro. Lily nodded and intensified her fire.

"This works because there's a crowd. If it was just the three of us, we'd still be targeted even if we were harder to detect."

"But with this many around, we blend right in?"

"Yeah, but at best, it just makes it 'less likely.' If we do too much damage or use Taunt, it'll still target us."

"I'll bear that in mind."

And since other players would attack regardless, this was definitely more a PvE skill.

As they talked, more Rapid Fire guild members came running in. Unlike the randos already assembled, they were organized for group play, protecting the back line or adding to the damage done.

"You're here! That should make things easier."

"But it certainly has a *lot* of HP."

"Yeah, this thing is clearly way tougher than any boss. Assuming that's not a design flaw, we've gotta figure it's meant to be fought by larger groups."

With Rapid Fire drawing aggro, solo participants had an easier time contributing. Their overall damage was rising. Members of larger guilds had called for backup, and other players had spotted the crowds converging. Others had done what Lily had, encouraging them to join the fray. With this many players hitting it, they were now making a solid dent in HP that had once seemed unreasonable.

Still, any monster this powerful was not about to spend the entire fight swinging tentacles around. It soon entered the next phase.

The squid floated upward and sprayed ink at the ground below. This spread out like a smoke screen, blocking their vision despite the lack of water around.

"This means...Lily!"

"I know! Retainer Rampart!"

Lily waved her flag, and her summons crumbled, re-forming into massive walls. No sooner had this sprung up before the three of them than there was a roar, and a wave smashed against them, shattering the ramparts. The water swept the ink away, but that smoke screen had served its purpose—hiding the start of the wave.

"An AOE when surrounded—smart move."

"Oh dear. Given the scale of the ink, it'll have hit everyone."

"I'd like to make it flinch and buy them time to recover..."

"......Well, good news. That should be possible."

They looked at Kanade, who pointed to the reason. Above the hovering squid was a flying turtle and three figures falling from it, bathed in a glow.

Wilbert figured it out first.

"That's Maple…and your twins? Um, what are they wielding?!" Despite their falling speed, Wilbert's eyes caught them slamming their weapons home. Maple turned her arm into tentacles, ripping chunks off the squid and swallowing them. On either side, Mai and Yui each slammed eight hammers home. DPS tenfold what any other player—even Wilbert—could produce. This generated a legitimately unnerving number of damage sparks and tore a visible chunk out of the squid's HP, slamming the boss back down to the ground.

Meanwhile, on Syrup's back, Sally, Kasumi, Iz, and Chrome all watched them dive. Making sure they were still in range of Martyr's Devotion, they prepared to make their own jump.

"Octo-wielding is nuts! Their DPS is off the charts!"

"And they buffed up first. You can add more STR to a weapon than you can an accessory, especially if it's a two-handed weapon."

Iz nodded, pleased with herself. With the damage they were doing, the weapons she'd provided were clearly worth the work that she'd put into them. You were only supposed to equip *one* hammer, so each could provide a substantial STR buff—this applied to *eight* at once was totally broken. And since the twins had skills that multiplied that…well, this outcome was inevitable.

"Still…they said they'd drop first and make the squid flinch, but I didn't think it would actually survive them."

"Yeah, a sight for sore eyes. A creature that can stand up to the hammer sisters."

Voicing their thoughts on this debacle, they followed Maple down, determined to end this giant squid for good.

Throwing the ultimate VS-Boss fighters—Mai and Yui—in

ahead with their DPS boosted to unprecedented levels? Why, that had instantly turned this fight around.

They'd brought down the monster, then landed on top of it. Maple kept them safe, so they just kept laying down the hurt. It might have withstood the first blow, but these weren't any sort of boosted ultimate moves—they were all just the twins' *regular* attacks.

Their bonkers damage had also stopped the squid from generating more waves, which gave the survivors a chance to come back in swinging.

Not about to waste this opportunity, everyone pulled out their biggest guns. But the most spectacular damage spray belonged to the members of Maple Tree, astride the downed squid.

"Mm, my guild always comes through," Kanade said.

This squid fight had started with just the three of them. Now it finally exploded into light.

With the battle over, the survivors came together to discuss the implications. Maple Tree members gathered around Kanade.

"Thanks," he said. "And sorry for the urgent call."

"No prob! That was surprisingly tough!" Maple replied.

Lily joined in. "We're the ones surprised. Your guild doesn't stand still."

Her eyes were on Mai and Yui and the extra hammers floating around them. Eight each, a downright arresting sight.

"Heh-heh-heh! Our hard work paid off!"

"If…you say so. That's not a feat anyone else could manage."

"Indeed," Will chimed in. "When I first saw you octo-wielding, I couldn't believe my eyes."

Mai and Yui had been mostly on the fifth stratum, getting used to controlling their new weapons. Since most of the player base generally focused on the newest floor, few people had seen them at this.

And the freakish sight was producing murmurs, yelps, and gasps from all around.

At that point, a message from the admins appeared, explaining what this giant squid had been.

"Ah...so that's why the event was designed to run so long. Makes sense."

"Giant bosses?"

"Stage two. The bulk of the second half will be fighting these raid bosses. Looks like that's not all that changes but clearly the main thing."

Lily and Sally had already skimmed through it and helped bring Maple up to speed.

With half the event remaining, players who had killed enough event monsters now had a new objective—defeating massive bosses that spawned on every floor.

Like Lily said, these were obviously not meant to be defeated by individual parties. They appeared at set times, in set locations, and every player in the area could join the fight. If they were not defeated within a set time frame, they'd vanish—encouraging the player base to be aggressive.

"And the number of them we defeat will affect the medals given after the event ends. Plus, they drop unique materials."

"Wow! That sounds worth the effort!"

The fight they'd just had was unique, triggered as the total event monsters slain hit the final reward. A lot like the fight triggered when Kasumi reached the center of the fourth stratum town. It had been pure coincidence that Kanade and the leaders of Rapid Fire had been standing nearby.

"We'd definitely appreciate Maple Tree proactively joining these fights. DPS is everything against bosses of that size. The twins will be an asset every time."

This praise made Mai and Yui blush, but it was an accurate assessment. Few things could ensure a successful kill more than them.

"Monsters that size are big targets and easy for them to fight."

Like Kanade said, this boss hadn't been that agile and was unlikely to dodge their swings.

Either way, the fight was done, and they'd just have to wait for the next one.

"Seeing how they've grown was an unexpected windfall. Will, let's gather our guild and head back."

"An excellent suggestion."

"Uh, see you at the next raid?"

"That would be nice. Later, Maple Tree."

With that, Lily and Will sauntered away. Everyone had assumed the rest of the event was smooth sailing—but now there was a new phase. Maple Tree got ready to throw themselves back in.

CHAPTER 6

Defense Build and the Flame/Storm Alliance

As the event's back half got underway, Maple was resting in the sun on a quiet seventh-stratum hill. There might be new bosses around, but given the numbers required, the raids were all scheduled, and the players were free to do whatever they liked the rest of the time. Plenty of players were still out there grinding the regular event monsters for their drops.

Iz had said they'd gathered enough materials. It never hurt to have more, but they didn't need to go out of their way.

"It's nice to just relax! When they speed up time for an event, we can all work hard together, but I wouldn't want to be like that all the time. Right, Syrup?"

Maple patted her turtle's head. Since this was a co-op event for the whole player base, she'd been going with the flow and fighting as the mood struck her.

She knew when the next boss would spawn, and the location wasn't hard to get to. Maple might not have a horse, but she could ride Syrup—getting there would be easy enough.

Then she just had to be a tank and keep Mai and Yui alive. The clearer her role was, the better.

She sunned herself a while longer, but then a huge shadow passed overhead.

Wondering what it was, she squinted—and the shadow reeled around, coming in for a landing.

"Hey, Maple. How's the event treating you?"

"Mii!"

The mage leaped down off Ignis, taking a seat beside Maple.

"Pretty good," Maple said. "We've got these raid boss things? So I'm just waiting for the next."

"The event monster grind is all over and done, yeah. You already got enough drops, then?"

"Yep! Eh-heh-heh, but it was mostly the rest of the guild. I guess I did help clean out some monster houses!"

Sally and Kasumi had done the majority of the work for sure. When they had the numbers, they used Velvet's trick and gathered drops in monster houses—and Maple had definitely contributed there. If you wanted to feel safe when surrounded by monsters, Maple was your best bet.

"My guild also put in a solid effort. Wasn't the best event for me, but I did okay."

"I knew you would!"

All the monsters in this event were water types, and Mii was all about fire—not really the best matchup. But at this point, Mii's fires could consume any trash mobs, even if they were her worst element.

"Mm, and it sounds like this event is gearing up for the eighth stratum. Which might mean I'm in for some rough days."

"That could be true. It might be all water!"

"Not sure how much these monsters count as a dry run, but if the raid bosses are all that element, I'd better get used to it."

"I'm not great with water, either. I can't swim! And I don't think I ever will."

"So that rules out all underwater fights? Well, if I ever have to fight you, I'll wait underwater."

That would also make it hard for Mii, so it might not help. But if she baited Maple down there, Maple would certainly not have a good time.

"But I guess I can swim by making my feet blow up!"

".........? *Is* that swimming?"

Whether by land, sea, or sky…Maple was a big fan of rocket propulsion. That just reminded Mii how weird this girl was, but she also knew that Maple had made blowing herself up a viable combat tactic.

"If only it did damage to you!"

"Heh-heh-heh! I'm too tough for that!"

Maple's defense was exactly why self-destructs could be considered a viable form of transportation. Mii could technically do the same thing, but her HP wouldn't last long, so the risks weren't worth it, and she couldn't chain the blasts well.

"I've got Ignis now, but if I couldn't at least match your rocket flight mobility, these raid bosses would shut me down."

This was why so few players leaned into their builds or succeeded when they tried. Mobility, durability, and DPS—there were all sorts of problems that cropped up.

"Syrup also makes it easy for me to drop in on things, and Martyr's Devotion keeps Mai and Yui safe long enough to knock everyone out!"

"I heard from my guild. Eight hammers now? They can knock out any raid boss with that."

"They almost managed it with the squid!"

"Yikes. That's nuts. I'd better warn my guild's tanks…"

Anything that hit so hard they could ignore the intended strategy on a raid boss was not possible for a *human* to withstand. They and their shields would likely disintegrate.

Mii and Maple chatted awhile longer. Maple had been kicking back to begin with, and Mii wasn't in any hurry. Both planned on joining the next raid, and Maple Tree had always planned to meet up at that location, so they figured they'd head in together. It was a decent distance away, but with Ignis, they could get there much faster than Syrup's backdoored bobbing.

As they were trying to figure out how to while away the time, a familiar face passed by. She spotted Maple and Mii, waved, and came over.

"Hello, Maple. And you must be Mii."

"Oh, Velvet!"

It sounded like she was in elegant mode today. Her usual challenging, lively character was replaced with a reserved facade. Mii cleared her throat once, then responded.

"Hmm, if memory serves, we've yet to meet."

"Right you are. But you are rather well-known."

"As are you. Word has reached my ears."

Fully aware of what they were both up to, Maple just watched their performance. "You're on your own today, Velvet?" she asked.

"Hinata had business elsewhere. I oft refrain from playing at such times, but I rather fancied a look at these new event raids."

She was trying to keep herself together, but clearly inside, she was chomping at the bit, eager to throw down. For anyone who knew what to look for, she wasn't doing a great job keeping it hidden. The grin kept slipping out.

"But the raid's quite far from here?"

Velvet had a horse, but the raid was still quite a distance away. The way she was acting, no way she wasn't planning on joining in—so why wasn't she waiting closer by? Maple looked puzzled.

"Heh-heh, we've still got time. Someone in my guild told me about something curious; I thought I'd take a look at that first."

"Curious how? Is it near here?"

Maple had explored this area before but hadn't spotted anything of note.

"Any ideas, Mii?"

"No, nothing that springs to mind."

"In that case…you wanna c— Uh, would you like to join me?" Velvet suggested, brushing off her slip with a smile. Mii had heard about this from Maple, and this served as another reminder of how she'd grown trapped in her own performance.

"I had no other plans. If we can still make the raid, I shall accompany you."

"If Mii doesn't know about it, I'm interested!"

"Then that settles things! Naturally, we'll be in time for the raid, too. I'm, like, hella ready to go!"

""Ah.""

"Oops…heh-heh…I'm rather eager to join in myself."

"…………"

Velvet was just smiling away again. Mii shot her a look of envy. This could have been her in a different timeline. Either way, they'd agreed to check out Velvet's "curious" lead, so they followed her across the field.

Velvet took them to a totally ordinary dungeon. Maple hadn't been through this one, but she'd known it was there. The entrance was a cave on the side of a hill—not at all hidden, not exactly a new discovery.

"Here?"

"Flame Empire members have already cleared this. If I recall correctly, there was nothing remarkable about it."

"Then you'll see when we get there! Though I hear luck is a factor."

"We have Maple with us. Luck is guaranteed."

"Ohhh? Y-you think? Fingers crossed!"

Maple offered up a silent prayer, and they headed inside. Generally speaking, if a dungeon was easily found and easily reached, the monsters inside were relatively weak.

Whether that weakness came from low HP or how many skills they had was another factor—but this place definitely didn't have anything of note.

"Martyr's Devotion!"

Maple used her skill to keep the two attackers safe, and that alone eliminated all threats from the slimes and golems—buffed palette swaps of old mobs. Now all she had to do was watch as the other two slaughtered everything.

"Allow me to pave our way there. No need to tackle them individually. Blue Fire!"

True to the skill name, blue flames scorched the rock walls ahead, lighting up the gloomy cave. When they subsided, all monsters in their path had been reduced to ashes.

"Wow! You're amazing, Mii."

"Noice! Ahem, I mean, excellent work. I look forward to fighting you and Flame Empire someday."

"......I can't exactly say 'anytime,' but if the occasion should arise, we'll hold nothing back."

"I should hope so. You've got a good guild, but mine's no slouch, either."

Flame Empire had made a name for themselves long before Thunder Storm, with a number of standout players among their ranks. Several of those players had caught Velvet's interest. Had she joined Flame Empire herself, she could have sparred with them on a daily basis.

"......I envy you sometimes, Velvet."

"Huh? Like, why? Whatever for?"

"......Best left unsaid. Some things are hard to speak of."

Mii gave her a sidelong glance and then burned up some more monsters.

"Huh, this a guild thing? PvP-related?"

Velvet's guess was fairly off the mark, but they were making smooth passage through the halls.

Then Mii stopped, spotting something ahead.

"Was this dungeon always so *damp*?"

"Huh? It wasn't?"

Maple had never been here before, but it wasn't how Mii remembered it. The farther in they got, the more moisture was on the walls and the more puddles they stepped in. Mii was charbroiling the event monsters before they could spray any water around, so that wasn't the source.

"Looks like luck's with us! Your prayers were answered, Maple."

"I doubt that! But I'm glad this worked out."

"This humidity... There must be something producing this water."

"You sure think fast! I planned to keep it under wraps till the last minute... Good instincts."

The gig was up, so Velvet explained what was so curious here. The raid bosses were not the only change wrought by the back half of the ninth event.

"Not sure if this is a stealth addition or what, but some dungeons have a chance of an alternate boss."

"And they're like the event monsters?"

"You got it! Ergh, I mean, that is so. But nobody has yet to work out just what dungeons are affected, what the odds are, or what drops they might have."

Velvet only knew about this dungeon because members of her

guild had happened across it. They'd only made a few runs at it, but so far it seemed like the encounter odds weren't very high.

"There's not much left to this event. We hardly have time to investigate every dungeon."

"There's a *lot* of dungeons and no guarantee you'll get lucky!"

Perhaps Maple's prayer had been answered. Scoring on their first attempt was very fortunate.

"But if this can happen, it might be worth running dungeons during downtime!"

"Indeed. That may be more profitable than grinding event monsters in the wild."

"If it seems like a secret, hard to believe there's nothing to it."

As they talked, they were trouncing monsters in their path. By the time they reached the back, there was so much water, every step they took made splashing sounds.

"What've we got?"

"I'm assuming it'll be water- or ocean-themed—maybe an extra-large version of one of the event monsters?"

"Should I open the boss door?"

"At your discretion."

"I'm ready!"

Making sure Mii had topped up her MP, Velvet flung the doors wide.

Beyond lay a giant jellyfish, wafting gracefully through the air. Clearly not the normal boss—and Maple's eyes gleamed at the sight of it.

"It's bobbing around! It's kinda cute."

"Word is, it's pretty tough."

"Then we must go all out. Flame Empress!"

"Same. Thunder God Advent."

Flames and storms flanked Maple. More than enough

offense—so Maple figured her role was to handle unexpected actions on the boss's part. If it had a way of getting through Martyr's Devotion, she was in trouble, so she kept all her summons up her sleeve, not even deploying her weapons, focusing entirely on defense.

"Flare Impetus!"

"Electromagnetic Leap!"

"Cover Move!"

All three used skills to propel themselves forward, closing in on the jellyfish. It responded with a ton of skinny tentacles, but that was just placing itself in danger.

"Eye of the Storm, Thunderbolt Alley, Lightning Rain!"

"Karmic Fire, Scorcher!"

Velvet produced immense amounts of electricity and Mii every bit as much fire. The tentacles were burned right off. Both girls were great at blanketing an area, and tentacles reaching out to snare them were ideal targets.

Maple made sure they both stayed in range of Martyr's Devotion and threw out Saturating Chaos, adding to the assault.

With its tentacle interference a failure, the jellyfish could not prevent their approach. Wreathed in lightning, Velvet stepped in. Mii hung back a step, slamming it with Flame Empress's fire spheres.

With its HP in free fall, the jellyfish lowered tentacles into the wet ground. Figuring that meant it wasn't going anywhere, Velvet and Mii both prepared to lay into it more.

But the water levels suddenly rose to knee-height. Not only were there regular tentacles to deal with—the surface of the water itself was forming tentacles. And when they got in the way of Velvet's lightning or Mii's flames—the player attacks vanished.

"AOEs aren't gonna help here!"

"Then lemme shove a fist up its ass!"

Velvet had *entirely* forgotten about staying in character. Leaving sparks in her wake, she rocketed forward. No longer able to burn off the tentacles, she watched as they rushed at her, grabbing her body. Like real-life jellyfish, this applied poison and paralysis and likely more damage beyond that—or would have, if Maple allowed it.

"Don't worry! It can't hurt you, and the poison won't work, either!"

"Thanks! Then—Purple Bolt! Double Whammy!"

A massive bolt burned off the tentacles, and she followed that up with two heavy punches. Those, too, were electrically charged, and each tore a chunk off the HP bar. Mii didn't even need to get close—she could remotely control Flame Empress's fire spheres and needed merely to fling them around from a distance. Larger AOEs were still effective; while it hurt to have the tentacles blocking them, they still had more than enough skills capable of downing this jellyfish.

Meanwhile, if the jellyfish's tentacle grapples were rendered moot, there wasn't much it could do. The whole design here hinged around tentacle quantity and status effects to immobilize its foes.

And Maple had ruined all of that.

"Get 'em, Mii! Velvet!"

She may not have worked that out. Maple was shoring up defenses, keeping her shield up, ready to use more damage-reduction skills.

But since she'd already nullified all the boss's means of attack, their victory was destined to arrive before she could take further action.

The tentacles' status effects were the boss's sole means of shutting down close-range fighters bringing the pain. With Maple negating that strategy, it was just a punching bag.

The jellyfish's HP hit zero, the water tentacles collapsed, and the boss burst into light—leaving a number of materials and three jellyfish behind.

"That was, like, way easier than I thought! Oh, uh...probably 'cause you two were both badass."

"Yes, bosses that can't get through Martyr's Devotion tend to work like this. I've fought alongside her several times and learned that all too well."

"I'm glad I kept you safe! Um, so we beat the boss, but..."

Maple poked the jellyfish it left behind, wondering if they counted as monsters.

"Those are not monsters," Velvet said, back in character. "They're trophies you can display in your room."

Guild homes had private rooms for all members. These jellyfish were essentially furniture items.

"Oh, so you put them in an aquarium?"

"My guild members said they fly around."

"They fly?! I guess the boss was bobbing about, too, and most of these event monsters are swimming through the air."

These weren't tamable monsters, but it sounded like one secret feature of this event was bringing home decorative mini versions of the event bosses.

"Then one each!"

No one argued with that, and they each picked one up.

"Some of my guild's members keep running dungeons, trying to collect these."

"Oh yeah? I guess I get that."

"Yeah! A bunch of them could give a room great vibes!"

Having defeated the secret boss, the three girls left the dungeon. Velvet looked a little disappointed, but she had the raid boss to look forward to. Mii's mind was on other creatures she'd like to decorate her room with. If these miniature monsters were exclusive to this event and couldn't be obtained later, then Maple planned to spend the rest of her free time running dungeons.

A few days after their dungeon conquest, every raid boss had been utterly demolished.

"Looking it over just shows how strong the players are."

"Yeah, I thought we'd set the HP too high, but maybe it actually wasn't high enough."

The developers were looking over the raid boss stats, reviewing the feeds of their defeats. The giant squid that had served to announce this new feature had caught the players unawares and given them a run for their money, but ever since then, they'd been trouncing everything. Since the players knew where and when the squid would appear, they had the monster surrounded from the get-go and could pile on.

The only reason the squid had lasted so long was because there'd been no focused fire in the early phases.

"Let's hope the rest of the bosses can cut it."

"Yeah...if they go down too easily, they aren't really worth calling raid bosses."

But they also knew the cause of their untimely demises lay with a very small number of players. Each of which had the strength to change the very course of battle. Even without them, with each stratum they added, more players were finding oddball skills. These players might not be game changers solo, but get enough of them together and they could do some real damage.

"I guess we keep fiddling with HP and defense?"

"Yeah, well…they were always designed to get steadily stronger, so that shouldn't feel off."

The players were working together, using their numbers to tear through each boss's HP—so the bosses needed stats to match.

"I thought this last one was overkill, but maybe not so much."

"Looking forward to it."

"Yeah, hopefully it'll be a good fight."

Perfectly aware that every previous hope had been trampled over, they shifted uneasily—and reviewed the stats again, letting themselves dream.

CHAPTER 7

Defense Build and the Apex of Authority

In the days leading up to the devs' last hope, Maple was having fun. She'd always been prone to chilling in-game, but thanks to the raid bosses and the mini-monster collecting, she had clear goals and enjoyed them as she felt inclined to make the most of her time. Now, she was at their guild home, showing off her mini-monster collection.

"I got this jellyfish first, but now I've also got this anemone, a clownfish, a manta, a shark, and a crab!"

She was lining them all up on the table in the main room. They were like quite detailed figurines and made the table feel like an aquarium.

"Oh, that's a lot, way more than me."

Sally added hers to the collection. She was in the same boat as Velvet—definitely down to fight anything time-sensitive, so she'd earned her share, but hadn't made it a priority like Maple.

"Quite a spectacle!"

"Yeah, players who are into aquariums must be pretty pleased."

"I can craft figures myself, but they don't move around like this."

"Please don't start creating life yourself, Iz."

"Well, I can't do that *yet*."

"But it feels like you will any day now, which is…impressive."

Figures that moved were different from miniature life-forms. Iz certainly didn't have the ability to craft her own monsters, so these were valuable.

"Too many to put in my room, so I thought I might leave them out here."

"It is relaxing. Hmm, maybe I should look for some."

"It almost seems like too few for a space this large. I've run some dungeons myself, but those rewards are not exactly common."

"I heard they're super rare!"

"They also drop from raid bosses. That's how we got ours!"

Raid-boss drops—materials or items—were distributed randomly to anyone who'd participated in them. Miniature monsters were on those drop lists. Mai and Yui were widely welcomed as final weapons against any raid boss, so they'd been fighting up and down the stratums and had far more raid-boss drops than anyone else in Maple Tree. That meant they'd gotten lucky a few times.

"It seems like they've managed to kill every raid boss so far. If we can hit the back-half target, that's five medals for everyone. We might manage to buy another skill before the next event."

"Oh! Then we've gotta help make sure these raids work out!"

The ninth event had been a long one, but the end was coming up fast. Maple Tree was motivated to help with the few remaining raids.

But Maple was planning on running dungeons again today.

"Where to?"

So far, she'd learned that each dungeon had a unique boss in it, and to her, it felt like some had higher spawn rates than others. The dungeon Velvet had taken them to had been that same jellyfish for her guild and their makeshift party, while hitting other dungeons had given Maple enough variety to fill the common room table.

"I'd like to get one of everything, but that seems hard."

Rather than try for dupes, Maple had been focusing on collecting a variety, so she planned to hit a dungeon she hadn't tried. Each one involved several runs to the boss room, so it made sense to pick dungeons that weren't too hard.

"Um… Oh! I know just the place!"

Her mind made up, she headed out of town, flying Syrup straight toward a dungeon.

She soon found herself at the colosseum dungeon—the one with all the stone statues. She and Sally had run it a bunch, and she had a solid grasp on the difficulty. Since it got harder the more players you had, she wasn't expecting a challenge while solo. It was a straight line to the finish, and the only other monsters were the usual event mobs. Ideal.

"I never expected to come here *this* often…"

She got off Syrup and headed in.

"Martyr's Devotion! Predators!"

It had now been a pretty long time since she first got the Predators skill. Since the monsters it summoned didn't level up, their attacks had started feeling rather feeble—but the Apex of Authority skill had given them a satisfying boost, and it once again had them dealing solid damage.

"Go get 'em!"

Maple brought the Predators to the first chamber, facing the stone statue. She wasn't sure what this dungeon's event boss was about, so she wanted to save all the skills she could. Predators was one of the few damage-dealing skills she could use over and over, and that stuck around awhile. As long as they weren't taken out, they'd just keep on attacking. And since Martyr's Devotion gave them Maple's defense, they wound up lasting far longer than they'd been intended to.

This statue had a club, and her two monsters were chomping on it from both sides. The statue was beating on them with the club, but Martyr's Devotion transferred all that damage to Maple, negating it.

"Okay! Now I just gotta wait here!"

Once she was sure this couldn't hurt her, Maple had Syrup lay down Red Garden, increasing the damage she dealt—then waited for the Predators to chew through the statue.

With no means of turning the tables, the statue did not have time on its side. It would fall eventually. The statue valiantly kept swinging, trying to hurt the Predators, but its HP slowly dwindled to nothing—and it shattered.

"Okay, one down! You really are much stronger now! Stat boosts make all the difference!"

Maple went and gave her monsters some pats, then headed for the next room.

Each chamber had one statue, but she had two monsters. That gave her a numbers advantage, and nothing here could defeat her. They chewed their way through the two remaining statues.

But when she reached the boss room, Maple realized this run was a bust. Previous dungeons had all started getting wet before the boss chamber. These secret bosses were hardly guaranteed, and she'd just have to keep trying until she got lucky.

"Okay! Then let's finish this boss quickly!"

She headed into the giant colosseum where the boss awaited, checking to see what it had to offer. It was a basic statue type—shield and longsword—and she looked relieved, certain she could handle it.

"Okay, let's do this! Syrup, Red Garden, White Garden."

Maple had Syrup use two skills that turned the field to her advantage, waiting for the boss to come to her. It swung that giant sword hard, trying to cut Maple apart. It hit her right in the head—and stopped dead, unable to progress any further. If it couldn't overcome this defense, then the size of the weapon didn't really matter.

"Next, Full Deploy, Commence Attack!"

Her weapons couldn't survive hits from that sword—so this was the prime opportunity to deploy them and add a barrage to the damage her Predators were doing.

If it blocked her bullets with the shield, that left it exposed to the Predators—if it tried to stop them, then it would be riddled with bullets. This was the clear difference between a boss that *had* to use its shield and Maple, who really didn't.

But by this dungeon's design, this boss was meant for one-on-one combat and could handle a fair number of play styles. Blocking her shots with the shield, it came charging at Maple. Even if this was a thrust, she was pretty sure it wasn't piercing; she just put her shield up and had Predators nip at its heels. Maple's eyes were on the sword—but instead, the shield came her way.

"Har?! ......Urgh!"

She was hit with a Shield Bash, which didn't actually harm her, but the body slam shattered her weapons, knocking her back hard. She bounced once, rolling away.

"Ah!"

And the knockback put Predators out of Martyr's Devotion's range. She scrambled up, calling them toward her.

The boss's sword started glowing red. It went into a spinning slash, slicing everything around it.

"Just in time! Pierce Guard! Heavy Body!"

The monsters barely made it back in range of her skill, and she quickly used skills to cancel piercing damage and knockback effects, weathering the strike. It was certainly a powerful attack, but she didn't really need to be worried about anything non-piercing.

"Okay! Can't let my guard down! Let's take this fight back!"

Maple redeployed her weapons and sent Predators back on the offensive. True to her word, she paid close attention, wearing the boss down. It never again got a real chance to hit her.

The statue's HP slowly drained away, and at last it fell to its knees. Assuming that was it, Maple turned to the exit circle...and only then did anything strike her as strange.

"Why didn't it vanish...?"

The statue's HP bar was empty, and it had fallen over—but not burst into light. Baffled, Maple moved closer, tapping it to see if it still lived.

"I *think* it's dead, but... Hmm? Is that water?"

There was a dripping sound at her feet...and a puddle spreading. When she and Sally had run this place, they'd spotted mystery water, too. As she remembered that—water shot up from all around.

"Whoaaaa?!"

Surprised, she backed off—and jangling chains rose from the water all around the statue. There were anchors on the chains, and they bound the statue, dragging it into the puddle as if the ground below it no longer existed.

This was like nothing she'd ever seen, and she watched with bated breath. The statue was soon replaced with a man in diving clothes and a run-down submarine.

Maple had fought a number of underwater monsters, but this was a first.

An HP bar appeared over its head, so Maple braced for combat.

"I bet that drops a miniature!"

Maple would love to add the classic underwater explorer. But this was too different from the norm, and she had no clue what it could do. She kept her wits about her, deploying weapons that were themselves a far cry from typical swords and sorcery.

"Commence Attack!"

When she started shooting, the boss dove into the ground, dodging. The water stopped spreading out—and began draining. Maple's eyes nearly popped out of her head.

"Huh? Augh!"

Just as she thought it was running away, water started gushing out right beneath her feet. Too late to react, she found herself trussed up in chains. Predators and Syrup were kept safe by Martyr's Devotion, so she had them stand by to attack and waited to see what would happen next. The ground at her feet flashed—and she was flung upward, hard.

"I-it exploded?!"

A giant column of water came apart, the spray raining down. The boss's attack had shattered the chains, too, conveniently freeing Maple. Ordinarily, that attack would have blown her apart, but in this case, it just blew her *up*. In the literal sense. And gave her time to regroup. Maple had Predators come back to her. If it was gonna dive around, then she'd take to the air on Syrup's back.

"Whew... So many surprises! But now I've got some distance!"

The anchors couldn't reach her here. Maple peered over the edge. The boss was regularly surfacing, and the water spread out just before it did, so it was pretty easy to tell where it would be.

The anchors popped out a few times, but like she thought, they couldn't reach this height. That seemed to prevent it from using the explosive attack, too.

"Guess I'll chip away at the HP from up here. I'm not very good at handling surprise attacks from below..."

She redeployed the weapons she'd lost in that last attack and shot beams at it when it surfaced. But these were blocked by a sudden watery dome, and while the vaporized steam was clearing, it dove back down again.

"I'm getting nowhere... This might not be my fight."

She'd yet to find an effective tactic, but since she was safe up here, she had time to think it through.

"If I have to attack when it's surfacing... Hmm..."

It had blocked the beams, so she could imagine regular attacks wouldn't do her much good. She ran through her skills and items, looking for anything worth trying—and one idea struck her.

"Okay, that should work!"

Maple scurried to the edge of Syrup's shell, got a good view, and stuck out her short sword.

"Hydra!"

She dropped a mass of poison on the ground, and it burst, transforming the area into a poisonous swamp. She did the same thing every time the cooldown ended, gradually filling the colosseum.

As she watched and waited, the ripples appeared below her poison, and the boss emerged. But this time—it was covered in toxic sludge. The status effect took hold.

"Cool, it worked!"

It was a gnarly visual but the best way she could think to damage her foe without getting hit herself. Each time it surfaced, it was poisoned anew, its HP gradually draining away. It had no means of reaching Maple up here, leaving it unable to do anything except poison itself repeatedly.

"Lots of enemies are immune these days, so it's nice to get one that isn't!"

The damage done wasn't that impressive, but Maple was good at waiting. Endurance tests suited her just fine. All she had to do was sit here—nothing hard about that.

"What else have I got?"

Leaving the boss to it, she looked through her inventory for some time wasters. She had puzzles like the ones Kanade played with, some decorations, and a bunch of food. She was always turning materials over to Iz or selling them, so half her inventory was devoted to entertainment.

She took out a few of these and laid back on Syrup's shelf, relaxing.

"I'd better do everything I can, though. Acid Rain!"

Toxic precipitation was the capstone of her strategy, a fresh new hell for the boss to face. Now she really did lie back and wait.

The boss slowly but steadily destroyed itself. Quite a lot of time passed before it burst into light.

Maple had spent the whole time lying back and playing with the stuff from her inventory, not even realizing the fight was over until she heard the boss shatter. She hopped up.

"Oh, it's over? Where'd it actually go down?"

She hadn't thought of that and peered over the edge. There was a puddle remaining where it had been, so she didn't have to fly all over the stadium looking for drops.

Maple moved Syrup over there, then jumped down, sloshing around in the poison. Soon, she found something *not* purple glowing in the muck and ran over. It wasn't a mini diver or a mini sub— but a strange black box the size of her palm.

"...How does this open?"

Maple gave it a look over, but it didn't seem like it would open on its own, and there wasn't any sort of keyhole.

"Guess I'll just take it with me!"

Didn't hurt to leave it in her inventory. As long as it didn't give her any weird debuffs, she could just take it home. And that was how Maple came to own the item named: Lost Legacy. Hoping she could get a mini submarine next time and wondering if there was a faster way to beat this boss, Maple left the dungeon.

CHAPTER 8

Defense Build and the Last Raid Boss

Maple busied herself with taking out raid bosses and gathering miniatures, but eventually it was the final day of the lengthy ninth event. And that meant it was time to conquer the last raid boss.

The members of Maple Tree had gathered at their guild home to prep and plan.

"These bosses have been getting steadily stronger. Safe to assume this one will be the strongest yet."

"Agreed. And it's the last, so they know almost every player will be there. If the boss is built to withstand that..."

It would have the HP to survive attacks from all directions and plenty of top-tier AOE skills. Yet this didn't really change Maple Tree's approach.

"Then let's do what we always do! Keep Mai and Yui safe while they pummel it!"

The twins had such high DPS, they could even melt raid bosses—no one else could match that. Maple and Chrome would be the core of their defenses. Kanade had some damage-negating grimoires, and Iz had some defensive items, too. Kasumi and Sally would be secondary attackers, tasked with clearing obstructions and deflecting incoming attacks. That would get them in range.

Once they were up close and personal, a nonstop parade of instakill-class regular attacks would annihilate the boss's HP pool.

""W-we'll do our part!""

This was a role only the twins could play, and they were fired up about it. They'd participated in a bunch of raids—It was no longer just Maple Tree banking on their DPS. If the hammer sisters were on your side, victory was guaranteed.

"Let's head out!"

Not wanting to risk a late arrival, they set out a little ahead of schedule, waiting for the raid boss to spawn.

The fastest means of transport for all eight of them was on Haku's back, so Kasumi had her white snake use Supergiant and carry them to the raid site. They'd been switching between Syrup and Haku based on the raids' locations, so by this point, everyone knew that if they saw a white snake, Maple Tree had arrived.

Some players went so far as to declare this meant they had the fight won. Anyone who saw the halo of hammers floating around Haku's head would likely reach the same conclusion.

Most players had seen the twins literally pulverize several raid bosses, and everyone knew they could trust those hammers to get the job done.

"Quite a crowd!"

"Yep. I thought we were here early, but looks like everyone had the same idea."

Throngs this large actively got in Haku's way. Kasumi had the snake lower its head so everyone could climb down, then returned it to her ring.

"No telling what this boss'll be. Best to put you away for now."

Haku's size meant its combat style was fairly nondeliberate;

ordinarily it just took advantage of its high stats to soak blows and strike back. It wasn't agile enough to dodge attacks—which meant it was best to know what they were dealing with before bringing it out. Even if she wound up not using her pet, Kasumi herself was much stronger now and had plenty of options.

Now they just had to join the crowd and wait for the boss to spawn.

Lots of people were planning teamwork with guild members, speculating what type of boss this one might turn out to be—and since Haku had been highly visible, other players came over to chat with Maple Tree.

"Like, the gang's all here! Can't wait to clobber this thing!"

"Hello. Velvet was eager to speak to you."

"Oh, Velvet! Yep, we'll all do our part!" Maple said, glancing around the faces of her guild.

"I can only do so much in these raids, so...if anything goes wrong, I'd appreciate you bailing Velvet out."

Raid bosses tended to nullify status effects, movement blockers, and skill sealers. Otherwise, no one would ever need a specialized build like Hinata's—they'd just have every player with a debuff spell hit the boss at once and render it helpless.

Meanwhile, Hinata's specialization really worked against her here; these raids had made her disappear into the woodwork.

"She puts herself down, but she's, like, doing tons of stuff. If Hinata lands a big one, you'd best take advantage of it!"

"Will do!"

As they spoke to Thunder Storm, more familiar faces approached.

"Hey, time for the final raid boss. Quite a crowd."

It was Lily and Wilbert. This time Lily carried the flag, and Wilbert was in butler gear, meaning she was their lead attacker.

"Looks like the bulk of Rapid Fire came," Sally said, looking past Lily. They'd been quite active in these raids, and she recognized a lot of faces.

"It *is* the last one. And…we're all expecting a doozy, yes?"

The puddle where this raid boss would appear was dozens of yards across, far larger than any before. It would be downright weird if this wasn't the toughest fight yet.

"That's right. Let's all bring our A game."

"I'm sure your guild has defense covered, so we'll have to make sure we don't accidentally die."

"Exactly. But I'm curious to see what they've got in mind for a crowd this large. Oh, Flame Empire and the Order of the Holy Sword are here."

Two big crowds had appeared in the distance. Even from here, they could see a dragon wreathed in light and the phoenix's fires, making it immediately clear which guilds these were.

All the top-level players had assembled here, making for the strongest possible raid party—now they only needed the boss itself.

"Shouldn't be much longer. Talk again if we all survive this?"

"Indeed."

With that, Lily headed back to her own guild, and Velvet followed suit, waving as she left.

"Almost time."

"Mm. Maple, defense is on you."

"You know it!"

Maple put Martyr's Devotion up in case it spawned swinging, and not long after, the pool began to glow, ripples spreading outward. Then a geyser shot up, and a muscle-bound giant emerged, wielding a trident and controlling the water around itself.

Everyone knew right away this was far more powerful than what had come before. As they boggled, a ball of water formed over its head, from which spawned a horde of the standard event monsters. An HP bar appeared over each monster's head—and the final raid began.

As the fight commenced, the boss thrust its trident to the sky. As it did, a flood generated around it, forming a tidal wave that rushed outward in all directions.

"Maple!"

"Pierce Guard! Heavy Body!"

Fully aware of her responsibilities, Maple went for maximum defense, meeting the wave head-on.

With knockback and piercing damage canceled, the seven guild members in range of Martyr's Devotion were fine—but the players around them were less fortunate. Anyone not in a party with Maple was left undefended, and players unable to weather the wall of water were swept away toward the rear.

"Everyone still here?"

"Thanks to you! Hell of an opening act."

Maple and Chrome had to double tank this party, getting Mai and Yui to the boss's side. With the water swirling around the boss, it was hard to see—but it *looked* like its waist connected directly to the ground, so it wasn't likely to move around. It made up for that with the orb of water above it, spawning hordes that charged down at the players.

This orb had an HP bar, too, so they'd have to take that out before the players could really flex their numbers advantage. As it was, many players were regrouping and engaging the incoming swarms.

"Okay, guess we're smashing that orb first."

"But from here, even Machine God can't reach!"

The wave may not have shifted them, but it was still pretty remote—for anyone swept away, that was doubly true. Even spells couldn't reach.

But there was *one* player capable of damaging that orb.

"Wilbert!"

"He can reach…? Damn!"

Lily's soldiers had formed a barricade against the flood; then they'd quickly swapped roles, and he'd drawn his bow. This had a far greater range than Maple's guns. His arrow a red bolt, his aim true—it pierced the heart of the water orb, yet did far less damage than they'd anticipated. It was going to take dozens of arrows. Given that each of his shots could one-shot your average monster, Sally found this downright strange.

"Does it nerf ranged damage? That would explain it."

"But it's so high up!"

"Wilbert, was it? Given the damage he's supposed to have, I dunno what else—"

"Hate to interrupt, but more incoming!" Kanade cried.

Everyone's eyes snapped up and saw the boss raising that trident once more. This time it summoned water spears, raining down from the sky above.

Once again, Maple Tree was fine, but cries went up from all around—the latest attacks delivered piercing damage. They were blanketing the ground so hard they were virtually unavoidable, but the twins would likely still struggle—so Maple couldn't afford to drop Martyr's Devotion.

"Gotta solve one problem at a time! Maple, no telling what this thing's gonna do, so you and Chrome don't have to worry about anything but defense!"

If they ignored everything else, two great shields would likely be enough to block all these water spears. As long as Mai and Yui were alive, they still had a shot at turning the tables. But first, they had to get through this. Was it better to take a risk and act or play it safe?

"What's the plan, Sally?"

"Gonna try and hit that orb. If I've called it wrong, I'll come on back."

She seemed confident, so Maple flashed her an encouraging grin. Despite the tidal wave, horde of monsters, and rain of spears—she was sure she could do this. That's what made her Sally.

"I'll come with, just in case. Anything goes wrong, I can back you up," Kasumi said.

Mai and Yui were all the DPS they *really* needed. Kasumi was the one guild member with AGI in Sally's league, and thus the only one capable of keeping up with her.

"Got it. Then let's move. This is starting to take its toll on the other guilds."

Maple had maintained their starting advantage, and they had to press that. Kasumi and Sally darted out of Martyr's Devotion, racing toward the raid boss.

And not just them—members of each guild had clearly decided they could not afford to focus on the adds. Each was closing in on the boss in their own style.

"Armored Arms! Blood Blade!"

As Kasumi ran, her blade liquified, attacking all enemies who drew near. She had a distinct advantage over Sally on range and lots of powerful skills that hit at the range limits. Sally normally made up for that with raw talent, but in this situation, Kasumi really got to shine.

"Don't worry about the mobs!"

"Thanks! I'll watch for the big guns!"

The boss had raised its trident a third time. This made a thin layer of water spread out, the surface of it bubbling here and there.

"Kasumi, this way! Stay on my tail!"

"Gotcha!"

By this point, Kasumi knew better than to question Sally's judgment. She matched step with her, and a moment later, geysers rocketed upward all over. Sally threaded their way through, closing in on the boss.

They were a mere ten yards out—but the orb was still dozens of yards overhead. Not something Leap would cover.

But the two of them weren't the only players who'd made it through the swarm and the boss's fearsome attack. Naturally, it was time to help one another.

"Sally! You're, like, a sight for sore eyes!"

"Velvet, Hinata!"

Sally had expected Velvet but raised a brow at Hinata. Somehow, she was floating along in Velvet's wake, towed after her—Velvet clearly doing all the work here.

"Never seen anyone do that!"

"I had Hinata tag along!"

"Looks dizzying. But no time to chat!"

They were here to smash an orb. Time spent on anything else was time wasted.

"Ice Stairs."

Hinata used a skill, and a spiral staircase wound around the boss—made of ice. Now everyone could gain the height they needed.

"Perfect! Kasumi!"

"Yeah, we'll make good use of it."

"We're coming with!"

Velvet dashed off—Hinata floating along via some gravity

technique—and Sally and Kasumi went with them up the icy stairs. Like she always did, Velvet had electricity coursing through the air around her, keeping weaker monsters at bay. For that reason, enemies were keeping their distance, using watery breath attacks. Three of them were nimble enough to dodge those blows even on this unstable footing. Hinata wasn't, but she'd ceded all control over her movements to Velvet and was keeping up just fine.

"Ice Wall!"

She was also blocking attacks with ice and gravity spells, helping all three out. There were other players starting up the stairs after them, but these four were the first to reach the orb. Velvet's primary element wasn't great against water, so their damage left much to be desired.

"Gravity Control!"

"Let's try Double Whammy!"

Hinata's skill made Velvet lift off the ground and move closer so she could punch the orb twice. Gravity Control was a gentle waft, and not exactly speedy—but at this range, that was just dandy.

But this did far less damage than she'd hoped; clearly, this was a *raid boss* and quite the HP sponge. It would take a while to get through that.

"Ugh, damn tough!"

"What now? Staying here, we can't dodge forever."

Velvet was floating near the orb, so her lightning aura was damaging the orb and the boss itself and instantly vaporizing any fish that spawned. That was all great, but Hinata's skill had a time limit. She couldn't keep the staircase or the hovering going forever.

"Gotta try everything we can! Velvet, watch out for monsters."

"I hear ya!"

Sally leaped upward, made some water of her own, and swam through it. This made dodging temporarily harder, so she'd asked

Velvet and Hinata to shoot any attacks down. She emerged above the orb and used a skill.

"Subzero Domain!"

The temperature dropped around her, freezing the orb underfoot. Unlike your standard ice-creation skills, this one could freeze existing objects. And by freezing the boss's orb, she'd turned it into a giant ball of ice.

"How's that? Quintuple Slash!"

"Vibrofist!"

"Final Blade: Misty Moon!"

The change of elements made it far easier for them to do damage. Three skills went off, hitting hard. Repeating this would destroy it in due time.

"It's working!"

"No, wait…Mind's Eye!"

Kasumi had caught glimpse of a blue light within the sphere and quickly used a skill that revealed where the imminent attack would land. An instant later—everything in sight turned red. The attack would hit it all.

"Shit, back off!"

Sally reacted first, and Velvet quickly followed. But with little footing, they were at a disadvantage. Before they could gain much distance, the ice burst from within, reverting to water—which swirled, watery blades shooting out in all directions. One hit meant death, so all four defended themselves.

"Oboro, Spirited Away!"

"Parry!"

"Ice Wall!"

"Third Blade: Blue Moon!"

They vanished from the map, physically knocked the attacks

aside, or leapt above them. Each did their best to avoid taking a hit, but with this many blades—they knew that was impossible.

But just as it seemed all was lost, fire and light shot it from both sides, instantly vaporizing the watery blades and saving them from certain doom.

Sally and Kasumi looked up to find The Order's leaders, riding Ray.

"Yoo-hoo! That looked dicey! We bail you out?"

"Didn't think you'd beat us here on foot."

"All those flying monsters really slowed us down…"

They looked the other way to see Flame Empire on Ignis. The other guild had bailed out Velvet and Hinata.

"Just like the last event. We saw you running off, but you were much faster than anticipated."

"You saved us again! Thanks."

"No problem. But we could use help, too."

"Ice, yes? I can do that. If we get close enough."

They'd lost Hinata's footholds but now had two flying pets— which worked just fine.

"I'll let everyone know to prep for attacks. Note, Pigeon Post."

The little yellow bird on her head flew off to the rest of the Order's members, and they waited for it to return. Mii's group was doing the same, killing monsters, circling, biding their time.

"Okay, good to go!" Pain said, signaling the Empire.

Ray dove in. Sally froze the orb again, and all twelve of them attacked. The scattered guild members had been warned of the coming freeze, and they'd spread the word—a huge volume of spells and skills came flying in, and the boss's HP dropped like a stone. Just before the boss's counter hit, the orb's HP was barely a dot left. It thawed and released a deluge of water, expanding.

Centered on the original orb's location was a swirling vortex of water blades. At the head of this, protected by what little liquid remained, was a blue core—clearly, they needed to shatter *that*.

The deluge was undoubtedly a big move it pulled out at low health, and it quickly bypassed everyone nearby, spreading out across the sky. The boss raised its trident, and the sky filled with water spears—far more than ever before. As if chastising players who'd been closing in, the ground, too, began to bubble.

No matter where you went, an attack was waiting. The force unknown, the range practically everywhere—Sally looked grim.

Mii and Pain concluded even their pets could not fly them to safety, and they tried to weather the hit with damage-reduction skills. But these skills applied only to their pets and members of their own parties.

"We're not covered…!"

"And this is gonna be a bitch to dodge!"

"I'll back you up however I can."

"Please. I'll do the same."

Marx created platforms and walls, and Misery deployed a field that reduced damage to everyone.

Shin and Mii got ready to shoot down as much as they could. The Order had Drag using rocks and Dread using a skill much like Sally's to give themselves footholds; Frederica and Pain were making barriers.

Sally had not expected this many skills for non-party members this fast, and she blinked, then glanced at the other three— the odds were against them, but they had to try and pull through.

They jumped off Ray and Ignis, landing on the platforms and bracing to dodge through the water spears.

Wishing they had a means of taking the core out, but well aware they'd have to survive this AOE first—Sally shot the core a baleful glance, knowing it had their number.

But before her eyes, a red light slipped through the gaps in the water blades and pierced the core itself.

Sally's jaw dropped—and half the water spears above them vanished. Much easier to dodge now. Only one man could have pulled off this feat, and silently thanking him—she focused on making sure no spears hit.

"Clean hit! Nice work, Will."

"Whew...well, I did what any archer should do."

Wilbert and Lily swapped gear again.

"You impressed, and now it's my turn."

"I can't wait. Take it away."

"You know I will."

Lily summoned a vast army of lifeless troops, preparing to have them soak the blows for players in all directions. Wilbert had done his part; now it was her job to keep as many players alive as she could.

"Numbers make all the difference. We've got an army assembled for this raid. Keeping them alive is simply prudent."

"Agreed."

With that, Lily's seemingly infinite troops stood in front of spears and geysers, protecting all the players in range.

"Wow, it's down already. I thought that would be way tougher."

"Looks like they're still with us!"

Iz was watching the giant's head through binoculars. The twelve fighters assembled there dodged through the incoming spears and then went their separate ways, descending back to ground level.

Maple Tree had (obviously) survived the onslaught without incident. Now it was their turn to go after the boss itself.

"If it looks like knockback or piercing are inbound, I'll cover you. You just keep on advancing!"

"Okay!"

Chrome could now protect several people at once with Multi-Cover. While Pierce Guard was on cooldown, Maple kept her shield up, and if anyone else looked ready to take a piercing hit, Chrome would block the blow—preventing Maple from taking damage. They were steadily closing in on the boss itself.

The destruction of the orb had stopped it from summoning hordes—but that made the tidal waves and geysers stronger, and it began swinging the trident around, attacking directly. Players were dying all over.

"Water spears coming! Cover everyone but me! Angel Guardian!"

"Okay! Multi-Cover!"

Chrome kept his shield over Mai and Yui, the guild members most likely to be hit. Maple and Iz crouched beneath her shield, blocking a spear with it, while Kanade used an Akashic Records skill to cancel the spears heading his way.

The boss's offense was dizzying. Spells and arrows came from range, while those with flighted pets used airborne hit-and-away tactics. Sally was with the leaders of the Order and Flame Empire, going between the ground and the air, making openings and racking up damage, but this *was* a raid boss, and they did not seem to have the manpower to down it themselves.

The game changer would be a break in the boss's onslaught, allowing the entire company to attack as one. And to get that—they needed Mai and Yui.

But the closer they got, the more intense the boss's offense became. More spears falling, fewer gaps between geysers, walls of water pushing them back.

"With Maple and me, nobody's taking damage, but this knockback is too much!"

Maple had Heavy Body, but that immobilized her entirely—and she couldn't negate the knockback at all while it was on cooldown. The shorter the gaps between waves, the more they struggled. They'd made it this close without taking damage, but that could easily go south if they changed tactics—forcing them to explore alternatives with great caution.

Then someone called out to them.

"Looks like you're struggling."

"Lily!"

"I'll make a path for you. Otherwise, who knows how long we'll be stuck playing defense."

Lily summoned more troops and ordered them to soak incoming damage.

"Go on, push forward. The sooner you can stop these obnoxious waves, the better."

"Got it! Come on!"

"Yep, that makes it doable. Thanks!"

With the troops guarding them, Chrome and Maple led their guild forward. They were almost in range now.

"I should be able to attack soon."

"Let's wait till they're actually there."

"Yeah, that'll let me provide support fire from the rear."

Lily and Wilbert watched her troops force a path for Maple Tree, waiting for their time to shine.

Surviving scores of attacks, weathering the big moves—and at last, Maple Tree reached the boss's base. Now they had only one thing left to do.

"Let's get you two buffed up!"

"I'll pile on every grimoire I can. If you don't down it, we'll be in trouble."

"Yeah, the rest is yours! Hit it hard!"

"Good luck!"

The effects didn't last long but were all the stronger for it. Each buff made Mai's and Yui's damage soar. When all possible buffs were applied, they were surrounded by disparate auras, pulsing with power.

""Here goes!""

They took a breath and swung all sixteen hammers.

""Double Impact!""

A basic skill any hammer user learned. But the instant it landed—it blew all the water away, replacing it with an insane quantity of damage sparks. No matter how many times they did it, the sheer power was downright unnatural. This might be the final raid boss, yet they still tore an enormous chunk from its HP bar. It toppled over, catching itself on one arm, barely managing to brace the other half of its body with its trident.

To the rest of the players present, this was the clearest sign they could turn this fight around. Like the raids before it, proof that they'd landed a big one.

All players surged forward, and Maple Tree kept pounding, not letting it get back up. Sally and Kasumi finally joined them again.

"Maple! That went well!"

"Sally, Kasumi! You're still alive!"

"Got bailed out several times. What's the deal?"

"We're going all out!"

Both raised weapons, facing the wide-open boss.

When the boss lost its balance, Flame Empire had been the first to attack.

"Ha-ha! They were amusing."

"They came and went like a storm—literally."

Velvet had run off to her own guild, Hinata still bobbing along in her wake.

"They'll do their part! We must not let this opportunity go to waste."

"Yup, yup, let's do this. Splinter Sword!"

"Not much I can do… I guess prep for when it gets up."

"Go on, everyone! If it strikes back, I'll heal or resurrect you!"

Shin and Mii were strong solo fighters, so Flame Empire's four elites generally did quite well as a party—but their real strength lay in group battles and formations. That was where Misery's healing and Marx's traps really came alive. They'd made a formation right up against the boss, and that would allow them to keep attacking even once it got back up.

"Wen, Far-Reaching Winds, Invisible Blades."

"Flame Empress! Fire God Inferno!"

Shin and Mii both had support skills, too. Shin's skills expanded the area effected and added wind blades to the attacks of every player in that area. Flames spread out around Mii, drastically boosting the stats of everyone nearby.

Like Lily said, numbers were everything.

"Pile on!" Mii roared.

And everyone started swinging.

As Flame Empire attacked, the Order of the Holy Sword members were launching their offensive on the other side of the boss.

"Everyone's buffing like crazy!"

"Ha-ha, for once, we don't have to worry about defense! Feels good, man!"

"And who exactly is doing that *for* you?!"

"No time to argue. We don't want this thing getting up."

"Yeah, let's hit it hard. Ray, Palidragon's Grace."

"Umbra, Shadow Pack."

"Berserk! Earth, Ground Pike."

As they buffed or called to their pets, Frederica borrowed Notes's power, buffing everyone and nodding to herself.

"You go get 'em! If the buffs run out, I'll reup!"

As if her work here was done, she tried to kick back—and Drag yanked her up.

"You attack with us."

"Ugh, you work me to the bone! At least if it's this big, it won't dodge anything... Okay, big guy! Make like a target and get wrecked!"

Frederica spent a lot of time dueling with someone she couldn't hit, but with the multi-effects and Notes, she could cast a whole lot more at once—when she did it, the DPS was considerable.

"Pain, I'll transfer all buffs when the moment's right. You do your thing!"

"You know I will."

All those buffs on one man—an absurd skill at any time, and the more people caught up in it, the stronger it got. Today they were at peak power.

Pain's glowing sword swung through, the light of it practically scoring the sky itself—and cleaving the boss, too. As if in answer, *NewWorld Online*'s largest guild struck en masse.

As the other guilds surrounded and attacked the boss, Maple Tree stayed put in front, pounding away. They might have fewer members than the other guilds, but Mai and Yui were each worth a hundred, and the damage they did stayed in competition.

"We sure can't beat that."

"Not even worth comparing."

Kasumi and Sally were with the twins, hacking at the boss. Maple stood behind, Machine God's guns firing away. Iz had already thrown all the bombs she'd made, and Chrome and Kanade were doing their bit.

"Ain't nobody going to me for DPS, but you've got options, Kanade."

"Yes, which is why my doppelgänger's working so hard. Sou, Calamity Cannon. I'm just being prudent. And with the twins around, my damage is negligible."

"Just do what you can. Oh, the buffs ran out. Chrome, toss these STR boost potions on them."

"Sure!"

The eight of them racked up a lot of damage. They were almost done—when the boss righted itself, thrusting its trident at those who'd done the most damage to it—Mai and Yui.

""We've got this! Titan's Lot!""

The giant trident's tip clashed with each twin's eight hammers, and what should've hit them was entirely reflected back at the boss itself. With their STR buffed to the max, they were stronger than the raid boss itself and capable of parrying that trident. It had had little HP left, and now it was hanging on by a thread.

"Okay, everyone go all out!"

Maple kept shooting. Sally and Kasumi unleashed combos. Chrome and Kanade threw out what skills they could, and Iz held no bombs or attack items in reserve.

""The finish!""

The true stars of this raid swung their hammers one last time— and the giant exploded into light.

"Great work, everyone!"

The raid over, Maple Tree had returned to their guild home to celebrate the end of the event. Mai and Yui had been the stars and were blushing furiously in a sea of compliments.

"I was shocked when I saw you with eight at once..."

"Never imagined there'd be a monster where that *wasn't* overkill."

"Hard to know what awaits us in the future. Personally, I'd prefer there not be too many like that..."

Probably best if only raid bosses were so tough, they could survive the hammer sisters.

"Oh, the event's barely ended, but it looks like they're opening the eighth stratum."

"Wow, the eighth stratum! Um, this event gave us five medals, right? That means we'll have access to the entire new map?"

"Yeah, guess we'll find out what that means when we get there."

"What could it be like?"

"I think I've got a pretty good idea."

"Oh? Really?"

"Yeah, I've got a hunch, too."

Maple tried to get Sally and Kanade to spill the beans, but they brushed her off, saying it would be more fun to go see.

"But there's a dungeon to clear first."

"Yeah...technically..."

Iz and Chrome both shrugged, exchanging glances.

The boss? They didn't know what it would be but didn't see it standing up to Mai and Yui.

Maple Tree awaited the arrival of the new stratum, not the least bit worried about the dungeon leading to it.

◆□◆□◆□◆□◆

Time passed, and the eighth stratum launched—so Maple Tree hit that dungeon. The way in was a joke—with Martyr's Devotion keeping them safe, Mai and Yui just disintegrated all monsters outside the boss room.

"Okay, opening her up!"

"Mm-hmm, ready when you are."

"Yes, we've got them buffed up."

Maple took one look at how the twins were sparkling and opened the doors. Inside, they found a gelatinous slime-like creature. Fitting with the seventh-stratum style, it was a shape-shifter—a bit like Kanade's pet. Humanoid, beast, or forms far more monstrous— some forms would even let it fly or delve into the soil below. Each transformation changed its stats, skills, and strategies, forcing players to think on their feet. A powerful, versatile foe.

"Oboro, Binding Barrier."

"Haku, Paralytoxin."

"Sou, Sleeping Bubbles."

"Paralyze Shout!"

"Necro, Dead Weight."

A barrage of afflictions came out as soon as they stepped through the door. Given its many forms, the slime had many resistances, so only Necro's movement speed debuff took hold. But slowing it down meant it couldn't get away—and was forced to allow the twin avatars of destruction to approach.

""Destroy Mode! Double Strike!""

There was a snap—and mid-transformation, the gelatinous slime went flying—and vanished. All it had taken was a single attack. And before it had a chance to use any of its myriad skills.

"I figured it had at least a few damage reducers…"

"But its luck ran out the moment they weren't nulls."

"You are getting every bit as absurd as Maple."

"Amazing! One hit! Or…sixteen?"

"We did it!"

"Um…thanks for the buffs and status effects."

"Feels real good to knock it out that quick. Almost feel sorry for the boss."

"But if they hadn't been able to land the hit, that would all have been for nothing. Bosses weak against slow effects are a cakewalk."

"I'm sure it'll do better against other parties."

Maple was giving the twins high fives, while Kasumi, Chrome, and Iz held a pity party for the boss.

"Oh, right! Eighth stratum! Come on!"

""Yes!""

The three extreme build players ran off, and the other five followed, catching up as they burst onto the new map.

"Wow…!"

"Well, Kanade? Your hunch prove accurate?"

"Hmm…I didn't think it would be this extensive."

"Yeah, me neither. This is gonna be rough to explore."

Before them was a sweeping oceanic expanse. The town was built upon the roofs of structures once inhabitable, this process repeated as the oceans rose.

"Whoa, what a stratum! Swimming could make it tough."

"Yeah, if it's this deep—then hopefully there are assist items."

"Uh…the ninth-event monster drops let me craft a bunch of stuff for underwater exploration. I guess this explains why?"

If you could swim a little or had acquired and raised the Swimming skill, this might just look like fun. But once the joy of the new view wore off, Maple, Mai, and Yui were starting to worry.

With their builds, none of them met the conditions to acquire the Swimming or Diving skills.

"Wh-wh-what do we do?"

"Can we do anything?"

"Um…are we gonna be stuck on these buildings sticking out of the water the whole time?"

As they feared they wouldn't be able to see much of this later, Sally patted their backs.

"Don't worry! Plenty of people never learned Swimming. I doubt they'll suddenly make that mandatory. Though I bet it *is* an advantage."

She figured there'd be some alternative provided. That helped everyone relax and look forward to what this floor offered. They'd have to find out—after all, they'd only just arrived. They didn't know enough to reach any real conclusions.

"Okay! Then let's look around!"

Maple raised her fist high overhead. The eighth stratum was a sunken city. Buildings rising from the water and abandoned towns sleeping beneath the distant waves.

AFTERWORD

Hello to anyone who just happened to pick up Volume 11. And my deepest thanks to anyone who's been reading all along. Hi, I'm Yuumikan.

Moving right along, this volume brought something new—but not necessarily to the story itself. Those of you buying this may already know, but the Volume 11 special edition includes a drama CD. A rare opportunity to hear your favorite characters talk—well worth the price. Like the ads say, it's all about a detour Maple Tree takes. A glimpse of their lives outside the framework of the narrative contained within the pages of the novels. If that sparks your interest, give it a listen.

This volume is about a new event that deepens their connections to the characters added in Volume 10. All sorts of new skills— and Sally is always thinking about how to counter them in the next PvP event. Enjoying the anticipation, imagining how they'd match up against what skills they know right now—perhaps that's fun for her. But by the time it happens, Maple will likely be something else entirely.

I hope you enjoyed Volume 11.

* * *

By the time this releases, it'll be a new year—and a year since the anime began to air. How time flies. It feels like just yesterday they got voices. I'm sure more news about the anime sequel will emerge with time—keep an eye on the official channels.

It might have been a year since the anime, but it's been four years since I started the web version. My readers allowed me to keep it going as long as I have, and that sparks both joy and a desire to bring this story to a proper conclusion. I hope you'll be there to see it happen.

But for now, it's time we wrap this up.

Everyone! Please keep reading!

Your staunch support fuels the story's progression.
I hope each new volume will bring you new delights.
And I look forward to seeing you all in Volume 12.

Yuumikan